BROKEN SHELLS

PRAISE FOR MICHAEL PATRICK HICKS

MASS HYSTERIA

"Brutal horror. Raw. Animalistic. I couldn't put it down!"
- Armand Rosamilia, author of the Dying Days series

"Mass Hysteria is a hell of a brutal, end of the world free for all. A terrifying vision of a future gone mad with bloodlust, Mass Hysteria will haunt your nightmares."
- Hunter Shea, author of *Just Add Water* and *We Are Always Watching*

"Fun, horrible fun, from start to finish."
- Horror Novel Reviews

"It's fast paced, action-packed, and bloody. Really, almost everything a horror gore-hound could want. ... Undeniably talented, Michael Patrick Hicks shows evidence of a rather deliciously depraved mind..."
- SciFi & Scary

"Mass Hysteria was a brutal horror novel, which reminded me of the horror being written in the late 70's and, (all of the), 80's. Books like James Herbert's The Ratsor Guy N. Smith's The Night of the Crabs. There are a lot of similarities to those classics here-the fast paced action going from scene to scene-with many gory deaths and other sick events. In fact, I think Mass Hysteria beats out those books in its sheer horrific brutality."
- Char's Horror Corner

"I'm telling you now, this book isn't for readers with weak stomachs. It is brutal in all the right ways."
- Cedar Hollow Horror Reviews

"If you are an aficionado of author Richard Laymon, you undoubtedly will like this book. This is horror at its

bloodiest, guttiest and most shocking."
- Cheryl Stout, Amazon Top Reviewer

REVOLVER

"*Revolver* by Michael Patrick Hicks, however, takes the 'shocking' gold medal. A classic example of social science fiction … most gripping."
- David Wailing, author of *Auto*

"*Revolver* is one of those stories that, once I got over the initial shock of the subject matter and the sheer vulgarity of the content, I immediately had to listen to it a second time. … with all the political turmoil, particularly the attitudes against women, that the world is being exposed to right now. I think this makes *Revolver* all the more terrifyingly plausible."
- Audiobook Reviewer

"A lot of what happens in this story resonates with what we see and what we read in our very lives today. *Revolver* is a great story, bristling with tension, unflinching with its descriptions and thoughtful. I get the feeling that people who misunderstand this may need to perhaps take a long hard look at themselves in the mirror."
- Adrian Shotbolt, The Grim Reader

"*Revolver* is a perfect short story/novella to read right now. The political extremists are gaining more and more power and they aren't easily ignored anymore. *Revolver* tells the story of what would happen if we let this extremism go too far. And wow was it good. … *Revolver* is a big "what if" book that will leave you feeling raw and full of emotion."
- Brian's Book Blog

CONSUMPTION

"*Consumption* is one of the most horrifically intriguing novellas that I've read for quite some time....a quite different tale of horror that resonates feelings of dread and shock, very well written, some great ideas and some darkness around the invention of various culinary delights."
- Paul Nelson, *SCREAM Magazine*

"Your stomach will turn, your throat will restrict, and jaw will clench tighter than a bull's arsehole in fly season."
- S. Elliot Brandis, author of *Young Slasher*

"...wonderfully macabre! Cleverly thought out, I was both disgusted and excited by this tale. This a MUST read for horror fans."
- Great Book Escapes

ALSO BY MICHAEL PATRICK HICKS

DRMR SERIES
Convergence (Book One)
Emergence (Book Two)
Preservation (A DRMR Short Story)

Extinction Cycle: From The Ashes (Kindle Worlds Novella)

Mass Hysteria
Broken Shells

SHORT STORIES
Consumption
Revolver
Let Go
Black Site
The Marque

BROKEN SHELLS

MICHAEL PATRICK HICKS

HIGH FEVER BOOKS

BROKEN SHELLS
Copyright © 2018 by Michael Patrick Hicks

HIGH FEVER
BOOKS

First Edition: February 2018
High Fever Books
ISBN-13: 978-1-947570-03-0 (paperback)
ISBN-10: 1-947570-03-X (paperback)
ISBN-10: 1-947570-04-8 (ebook)
ISBN-13: 978-1-947570-04-7 (ebook)

Edited by Shay VanZwoll
EV Proofreading
http://www.evproofreading.com

Cover artwork by Kealan Patrick Burke
http://www.elderlemondesign.com

All rights reserved. This book or any portion thereof may not be reproduced or used in any manner whatsoever without the express written permission of the publisher except for the use of brief quotations in a book review.

This is a work of fiction. Names, characters, places, and incidents either are the products of the author's imagination or are used fictitiously. Any resemblance to actual persons, living or dead, businesses, companies, events, or locales is entirely coincidental.

Printed in the United States of America.

*To Maureen, Ben, and Jonathan,
who help keep my monsters at bay.*

ONE

LIKE MOST GOOD THINGS in Antoine DeWitt's life, it wasn't long before it got completely fucked up. His job as an auto mechanic had been going well, and had been the only real job he'd held since being released from prison two years ago on a possession charge.

Had been, right up until that dipshit redneck he worked with started talking about how great a president Trump was. "Better than," he said, looking Antoine straight in the eye, "that Nigger-In-Chief we had us before."

Twenty minutes later, the repair shop's owner threw Antoine out on his ass, threatening to call the police. The dipshit redneck had been left with a black eye and bloody, swollen lips that hid the gap left after Antoine knocked out three of the man's front teeth.

Bus brakes squealed loudly as the wheels ground to a halt. Antoine tiredly made his way down the steps, the pneumatic door hissing shut behind him. A thick cloud of carbon monoxide enveloped him as the bus groaned away from the curb, and he started walking the nine blocks to home.

Night fell quickly, and there were no streetlights in Antoine's neighborhood. Kids threw rocks and busted the lights, or gangbangers shot them out for fun, and eventually the city grew tired of replacing them. The kids and the gangs also liked to start fires, mostly because a gallon of gasoline was far cheaper than a night at the movie theater and provided just as much amusement. Antoine passed the burnt husks of fallen homes. Weeds were already starting to overtake the black carbonized remains.

His apartment was on the third floor of a battered brownstone. He climbed the loose, cracked steps, passed through the noisy, hinge-squealing front entrance—the doorframe of which was canted a good ten degrees off level—and stopped at the graffiti-tagged mailboxes. Most of what was in his mailbox was junk and bills, several marked as past due, and he thought about throwing it all away. Instead, he carried it up the stairs, already hearing his screaming baby before he even made it to his floor's landing. He closed his eyes, took in a deep breath, and slowly released it before stepping foot inside his home.

Inside the small apartment, Chanelle was smoking. Helix was in his crib, red-faced and crying as balloons of snot popped in one nostril.

"I don't know what to do with him," she said.

Yeah, that much is obvious, Antoine thought. He was too exhausted for another fight, but still knew better than to say those words out loud. He tossed the mail down on the beat-up card table they had picked out of the garbage ages ago and pretended was just as good as a fine dining table. She began rifling through the mail, complaining about Helix and life in general, but Antoine didn't listen. The lights were off, in the hopes of cutting down on the electric bill, so she skimmed the mail by the minor glow of a nearby nightlight.

"You feed him?"

"Of course," she said. "Tried to, anyway. He didn't want to eat. Don't want to be cuddled, neither. Nothing. He just wants to scream his fucking head off, so let him."

"You check his temperature?"

She snorted, smoke blowing through her nostrils. Antoine thought she looked like an angry bull. "Yes, I checked his fucking temperature," she said. The words were slow and measured, and he knew she was gearing up for a fight.

He turned to the crib and picked up Helix, rubbed his nose against the baby's. Helix didn't seem to like that much and redoubled his efforts to build up an even noisier ruckus, smacking at his daddy's face with a chubby hand.

"Hey, what's this?" Chanelle said.

Her eyes were lit up over the glossy car dealer's ad.

"It's junk," he said. "Throw it away."

Instead, she began picking at it. A flap was adhered to the front of the flyer, the words "Money Carlo" in oversize block letters and obnoxiously bright colors. It looked like an oversized scratch-off ticket, but with pull tabs instead of the gunk you had to remove with a coin that always made a mess of the table, and the promise that if you matched the numbers or pictures of fruit on the left side with those on the right side, you could win up to twenty-five thousand dollars.

Her nails slid under the tabs, popping them up one by one. The resolve on her face quickly slid into disappointment as she looked upon one loser after another. He bounced Helix in his arms, trying to shush the kid with a steady whooshing noise that was supposed to mimic comforting noises he had heard in the womb.

"Oh my god," she said. He turned to look, already dubious. "We won five thousand dollars!"

He rolled his eyes. "No we didn't."

"Yes, we did. Look."

He looked. Sure enough, second to last in the row of five chances were a pair of matching sevens. According to the prize chart for possible matches, that meant they'd won five grand.

He shook his head. "C'mon, Chan, it's nothing. It's probably how much they knock off buying a new car or something. Which we're not going to do. Forget it. It's a scam."

"It's five thousand dollars," she said, as if speaking to a slow child. "Honey, you gotta call this number, claim it."

"Chanelle, stop it. It's junk. Just throw it away."

Helix was screaming up a storm in his ear, and he bounced the baby more. His frustration with both of them was growing. On top of that, he had to figure out how to explain to her that he was now unemployed. He hadn't seen this month's WIC check in the mail yet, either, which was already three days late. They needed that money, or else pretty soon they weren't going to have any cash at all. Not one fucking dime.

So...what if...?

No, he chided himself. Chanelle was being stupid, and that so-called lottery ticket was just a scam. He knew all about scams, having met plenty of con artists while he was in the clink. The whole thing was a trick to get suckers in the door of the dealership and on the line to buy a new Cadillac or some other car they couldn't afford. The dealership would take whatever money they could and then, after the first payment was missed, would repossess the car and resell it to some other poor fucker. Bottom line, it was bullshit.

"Call the number. Please?" she whined.

He sighed. He was exhausted and aggravated, and he sure as shit didn't want to call anybody. He needed a beer and some quiet time on the couch.

Helix nearly wriggled his way out of Antoine's arms, so he set the child back in the crib. Then he sat down across from Chanelle and screwed up the courage to tell her what had happened at work. His asshole clenched imagining how it would go.

"I got fired," he said, not sure how else to say it. Straight, to the point—that seemed to be the best way to approach it. She stared at him with wide, googly eyes, and he went on. Told her about the redneck's big mouth and how he'd shut him up, and how that had been the last straw for his boss.

She slid the flyer at him forcefully. "So, see? You gotta call, Antoine. You gotta."

He'd been expecting fury and yelling, and his shoulders slumped in defeat. Had she even been listening? Instead, she was still on about the goddamn stupid ticket. Even had a curl of a smile on her face, like she'd just one-upped him.

"Channy, this is horseshit. You know that, right? You ever heard about how if it's too good to be true...?"

"Then it probably is," she finished. "Yeah, but what'll it hurt if you call and confirm?"

He stared at the wall behind her, watching the smoke dance toward the ceiling.

"If you're right, then we got nothing. But if *I'm* right," Chanelle said, "then we got five grand. Besides, what's your broke ass gotta lose?"

He pinched the bridge of his nose and slowly exhaled, trying not to show how hard her parting shot had hit. "Yeah. Fine. All right," he said, knowing he was doing this merely to appease her. To shut her up. He pulled a flip phone at least six years out of style from his pocket and punched in the number.

A recording greeted him and asked for his claim code from the ticket. He typed in the numbers, listening as the automated service made some kind of digital clicking noise while it processed the prompt for its next recording. He wished it would hurry the hell up.

Finally, the tinny robotic woman's voice said, "Congratulations. Your ticket has been identified as a winner. Please bring your Money Carlo card to the Dangle Chevrolet Dealership to collect your prize. And please stay on the line to answer a few important questions."

He waited, then was asked to pick from a selection of five choices on when he would be ready to purchase a vehicle. He hung up. His heart was racing, his mouth dry all of a sudden.

"Well?" Chanelle asked.

"Said it's a winner."

Chanelle clapped her hands and let out a whoop. "I told you! I told you!"

Antoine looked down at the flyer for the address of the Dangle dealership and their business hours. He recognized the name of the dealership and the street it was situated on, pegging it as being out in the middle of the nowhere. He would have to take the bus, and after that he'd be in for a good, long walk down M-72, right through the goddamn woods.

Who the hell would put a car dealership all the hell the way out there?

He knew the area well enough. M-72 was a stretch of highway that cut across Northern Michigan shore to shore. Much of the land it ran through were woods and agricultural areas, connecting a few small villages to the larger interstates. Dangle's was off the highway, and a good distance away from anywhere at all. *This Money Carlo crap was probably the only way they could get anybody in the showroom.*

"They're open till nine tonight," he said.

"Well, what are you waiting for?" she said, practically hopping in her seat. "Go get our money, honey!"

He still couldn't shake the idea that this was all bullshit designed to lure him into the car dealer's joint, and the last thing he wanted to deal with was warding off a pesky salesman trying to badger him into another monthly bill he couldn't afford.

He also couldn't shake Chanelle's argument, or—he had to admit—that small niggling part of his own mind that continued to ask, *what if?*

Besides, this was as good an excuse as any to get out of the apartment, away from the screaming, away from Channy's cigarettes. Barely finished with the one in her mouth, she prepared to light up another. And Helix, he seemed to be getting louder and louder. Maybe a walk would help clear his head.

Yeah, okay. Fuck it.

The chair scraped against the linoleum as he stood. Antoine pulled his carpenter's coat back on and slipped the flip phone back in his pocket.

"All right," he said. "I guess I'll go check it out then. But, look, don't get your hopes up on this, okay?"

She nodded, but he could tell she was already thinking of ways to spend the money.

Somehow he managed to convince himself, too, that this would be worth it. If Chanelle was right, then five thousand bucks was five thousand bucks, and they desperately needed the cash. Maybe something good would come of this. The day had been a massive clusterfuck, and, if anything, Antoine was owed a break.

Maybe even a five-thousand-dollar break.

TWO

JON DANGLE SAW THE black man approach from across the street, watching intently as the man walked through the parking lot and made a beeline for the showroom doors. The stranger seemed out of place even before he stepped inside and began looking around.

Dangle had been selling cars for more than a decade, and his salesman's eye told him everything he needed to know about the man immediately. Hoofing it into the lot like that, his posture bowed as if defeated by the entire world and gazing at the cars with discomfort, the guy was a laydown, an easy mark: either desperate for a car or had extraordinarily bad credit. Even at a distance, Dangle recognized the colorful, shiny Money Carlo mailer, and he knew then the man was a total laydown for sure.

From behind his desk, Dangle said, "Can I help you?"

"Yeah. I got this ticket in the mail. Called the claim number and got told to come in with it. Says I won five grand."

Dangle stood, plastering a large, toothy smile on his face. "Well, I'm happy to help you, sir. Let me see that now."

Dangle took the proffered ticket and spent a moment studying it. "Ah, yes. Matching sevens. That's good. That's great. This must really be your lucky day."

The man shrugged, his thick shoulders rising and falling. For someone on the verge of such an important moment, he looked strangely bored, oddly hesitant. Dangle understood. The customer was waiting to find out what the catch was, because there was always a catch. For men like the one across from Dangle, there were oftentimes even more than just one catch. Dangle fell back into his chair, inviting the mark to sit as well.

"I just need to see your driver's license," Dangle said, looking down at the recipient address on the flyer, "uh, Mr. DeWitt."

DeWitt shifted in the chair to free his wallet from his back pocket. He didn't have a driver's license and it took him a moment to get the State ID card free before handing it over with a shaky hand.

"Nervous?" Dangle said, still smiling.

"I dunno," DeWitt said. "Not sure what else I'm supposed to do."

"You just sit tight. I need to make a copy of this and scan the QR code on here." He flicked the card with his index finger in emphasis. "That'll activate the pre-paid debit card for you, and you can be right on your way. Or, please, feel free to look around and let me know what catches your eye. I saw you notice the Camaro on your way in."

"Yeah," DeWitt said. "It's a nice one."

"That she is," Dangle said. He took an appreciative look at the sleek, yellow sports car and its elegant curves. "Go take a look. I'll be back in a jiffy."

Dangle stood again, somewhat disappointed that DeWitt stayed seated. The dealership was dead and, with only an hour left until closing, he didn't expect that to change. Most of the day, in fact, had been spent rotating vehicles around the lot and playing musical chairs with the cars to create the impression the dealership was busier than it was. His father had instilled in him the same philosophy that kept the business going for more than two generations: action creates reaction. Sometimes it worked, sometimes it didn't. Today, it hadn't. Tomorrow, they would put out a couple hundred balloons and make sure the lot stayed busy as he and the other salesmen moved cars around.

He walked down the hallway to an Employees Only section, and down a corridor to a plain white door. He stepped through, pulling it shut behind him, and handed the ID over to the man, his brother Jensen, behind the computer.

A large bank of monitors showed a live feed of the showroom floor, and one of the security cameras had been positioned directly on DeWitt. The man's large, black face filled the screen. He was just sitting there, like a rock.

Jensen typed in the address from DeWitt's identity card, using the street-level view of Google Earth. The cached image showed a bright daytime scene of a run-down, clearly impoverished neighborhood. Dangle had noticed DeWitt's rough and cracked palms, clearly a laborer who worked with his hands. So far, things were looking good.

Black, from a poor neighborhood, likely in a job with high turnover, and plainly in need of quick, cash. Only those who were truly desperate came in with the Money Carlo cards, thinking they were going to make an easy payday.

A moment later, Jensen was pulling up DeWitt's criminal history through a pay site that allowed users to look up whatever they wanted.

"Busted for felony possession, did two years. Out on early release," Jensen said. Dangle nodded, smiling as Jensen pulled up the man's credit report.

"In debt to a lot of companies. Past due on credit card and water bills."

Jensen droned on, but Dangle was already way ahead of him. He could feel it. DeWitt was perfect. He was a fucking ghost, and even better, he was alone. Single, on foot, no vehicle in his name, underwater in debt, and nice little rap sheet to boot. He wondered what narrative the cops would create, if they were ever tasked with investigating the disappearance of Mr. DeWitt. A junkie looking to score, maybe, or just somebody who walked out on the life he'd had and disappeared. It happened all the time. The police wouldn't waste resources looking for him, not when they had murders to solve and rapists to catch. Or at least parking tickets to write. What would some ex-con who vanished in the middle of the night mean to them? Nothing. Absolutely nothing.

"I'm not seeing any social media profiles," Jensen added, clicking his tongue against the roof of his mouth.

Not too often did someone this perfect walk into the lot, but it happened on occasion. Hell, it was why he pulled the Money Carlo scam to begin with, in the hopes that he'd find a ghost just like this.

He waited until DeWitt finally stood, then gave him a few minutes to walk around and look at all the pretty cars that were well beyond his means before returning to the showroom.

THREE

BEING IN THE DEALERSHIP made Antoine uncomfortable. He didn't like being alone and surrounded by all these expensive vehicles. The white girl behind the receptionist counter wasn't exactly subtle in her observations of him, either. Her eyes followed his every step, as if she was waiting for him to make a single mistake. He nodded and smiled at her, and she returned the smile with a look like she had drank spoiled milk.

The bus had dropped him off in an entirely different world than he was used to. Restaurants and fast food chains and coffee shops lined the street, all lit up and still hustling, their parking lots full. Definitely not like his neighborhood of burnt-down homes and abandoned cars left to rot, and apartment buildings that were a good strong gust of wind away from collapsing. He couldn't help imagining some kind of silent alarm had gone off the minute he'd stepped off the bus. WARNING: BLACK MAN COMING! He snickered at the thought, which prompted the receptionist to further scrutinize him through narrowed eyes.

Once off the bus, he'd got to walking, his feet carrying him two miles past the edge of town and out into the sticks. The buildings tapered off down to a few sporadic houses, nature getting more and more prominent. He thought it strange that a car dealership would be so far off the beaten path, and wondered why they weren't closer to the village, or at least the highway exits. Sure, it was only a few miles outside civilization, almost smack dab in the middle of nowhere between Grayling and Kalkaska, but it still struck him as odd. Even as M-72 began cutting into the woods, he swore he'd felt eyes on him long after he'd put his back to the last house. People were watching him, he was certain, and he'd looked around for the cop cars he suspected were hidden nearby or, at the very least, would start rolling along behind him.

It hadn't been too far from this dealership, on this stretch of road, in fact, where he'd been busted a few years back for driving while black. A white cop had pulled him over, even though he had been going the speed limit, and said he'd run a yellow light that Antoine knew damn well had been green when he went through the intersection.

His license had been expired, and he did not have insurance. The cop crinkled his nose the moment the window went down and he took a number of exaggerated sniffs, letting Antoine know he smelled the weed. A short while later, Antoine was cuffed and sitting on the side of the road, flanked by officers from a second and third patrol car that had arrived on scene, watching as four cops rummaged through his vehicle. He had kept his mouth shut and cooperated fully. He knew the police would not need much of a reason to pop five rounds into his head if that was how they wanted the night to go, even though he was unarmed and the only thing in his car was weed. The officers had gotten rough with him while handcuffing him, but Antoine had taken it, refusing to give them whatever opening they were looking for. They could have beaten or killed his black ass on the side of that deserted road if they had wanted to, but he sure as shit wasn't going to do anything to provoke them. They let him live. The vehicle was impounded, and Antoine was hit with possession and intent to distribute. He hadn't had anywhere near enough weed to distribute, but he also couldn't afford anyone other than the court appointed attorney, so he simply followed the counsel's advice to plead guilty. For all he knew, whatever cop had weighed the bag of marijuana had left his thumb on the scale to artificially inflate the weight and make an otherwise minor arrest into a bigger bust. Antoine suspected that was the case, but he certainly couldn't prove it, and nobody had been interested in listening to or helping him anyway.

Now he was standing beside a sleek, freshly waxed Camaro. He ran his fingers over the smooth curves, appreciating it. He knew he'd never afford it, but it didn't hurt none to look.

Five thousand dollars. The figure kept dancing through his head. Yeah, if it sounded too good to be true, it probably was. But still. He'd expected the car salesman to wind him up with some kind of pitch, and he was still waiting for the other shoe to drop. So far, it hadn't. Maybe this was the real deal, then. Maybe he'd actually won some money.

He was trying hard not to get his hopes up. He fully expected the slimy hustler to come back and say, oh, gosh, so sorry, but this ticket actually isn't a winner, or offer up some other explanation about how the five grand is only for a down payment on a new car or how much they'd be willing to offer up in financing. Some load of bullshit, sure, but definitely not five large in cash, free and easy.

The gleam on the car was so shiny, he saw the reflection of the approaching salesman and turned.

"Ah, Mr. DeWitt, there you are," he said, as if DeWitt could have possibly been anywhere else.

Antoine rubbed his hands together. "Yep, right here. So, uh, what else?"

The salesman smiled. "Everything looks good, sir. Your card has been confirmed and you are, indeed, a winner. If you wouldn't mind following me back, there's just some paperwork I need you to sign and then you can collect your winnings."

"Back there?" Antoine said, pointing to where the man had disappeared to moments ago.

"Yes. It's a private office. I know there's nobody around out here, but still. It isn't something we want to show off, you understand? Not everybody can be a winner."

"Oh yeah," Antoine said, chuckling despite himself. "I know all about that."

"So, if you would, please," the man said, extending his arm for Antoine to pass ahead of him.

Antoine started walking, and caught the eye of the receptionist as he passed. She was a pretty little thing, and she flashed him a wide, toothy smile, a twinkle in her eye. Her display was fake as shit, but he smiled back anyway, feeling good.

"The second door on your right," the salesman said.

Antoine turned, the door opening smoothly as he pushed through. The room beyond was shadowed, but he could make out the interior from the hallway lighting. The walls were blank, and ahead of him were stone steps leading down.

"What the—"

A sharp jolt of pain bloomed in his neck. His hand went to it as he turned. His eyes widened and he tried to scream, unable to believe what he was seeing. He stepped backward, his foot landing wrong on the step below, and he fell.

His spine and the back of his ribs banged painfully into the stairs, and he tried to slow his descent but the stone walls were slick and even, too smooth to grab onto. He tumbled down, head over ass, limbs knocking solidly and scraping against hard edges. His whole body ached as he slammed to the dirt ground.

His head throbbed, his vision doubling, tripling, and turning foggy until he saw only darkness. A skittering noise against stone echoed around him, and he turned to find the source but his eyes stung and the world was so damn blurry.

Fresh pain erupted in his midsection. He doubled over, the scream dying in his throat as the world went black.

FOUR

ANTOINE SLOWLY CAME TO, but his eyelids were too heavy to budge. They felt glued together. He was fine with keeping his eyes closed as a thick grogginess clouded his head and he thought about going back to sleep. He thought about rolling over and putting his arm around Chanelle, snuggling up close to her and warming himself against the heat of her body.

When he tried to turn, his body refused. Something pressed against the length of him, and his limbs were stuck. That was when he noticed the bone-deep ache stretching across his entire body. His muscles felt heavy with exhaustion, filled with lactic acid that burned all the way through him.

His eyes still would not open, and he tried, desperately, to see what was happening. Panic welled up from deep within his belly, and he had to clamp his lips tight and swallow back the urge to scream. He was blind and trapped, confined in what he was quickly beginning to realize was a very, very tight space.

Reeling with sudden fear, he worked to calm his breathing and slow his heart.

What the fuck is going on? rang through his head with persistent abandon. *What the fuck, what the fuck, what the—*

He forced his mind to quiet, drew in a long, deep breath, held it for a three-count, and then slowly released it over the span of five seconds. He repeated this process several more times, until he felt some control ease back into place.

Although he couldn't see, he could at least get some idea of the state his body was in. He wriggled his toes, but his feet or legs were otherwise immobile. There was a bit more leeway with his arms, but not much. His left arm was trapped between a scabrous material and his coat. His right arm was pinched against his side. Antoine could not tilt or turn his head, and his shoulders were pinned.

He moved his left hand, sucking his belly in, and felt the belt loop of his jeans beneath the coat. If he could reach his right hip pocket and free the knife he carried, he might be able to cut his way loose. With his shoulder locked in place, though, any kind of movement was difficult. His muscles throbbed, and pulling his stomach in only served to amplify the pain in his abdomen. The tendons in his shoulder were taught, stretching uncomfortably as he inched his fingers closer to his pocket. His forearm slid slightly, but not enough. The exposed skin of his hand and wrist scraped against the hard substance locking him in place, and notes of panic bubbled up within him once again. He scrunched his already closed eyes shut even tighter, forcing his arm to reach and maneuvering his fingers into his hip pocket. With his middle finger, he could feel the edge of the blade's pearl handle— just as the knife slipped deeper into his pocket.

He wanted to shout all of the profanity he knew, but instead he gritted his teeth and let loose an angry, frustrated grunt. A tapping noise met his choked grunt, followed by the sound of something skittering rapidly across rock.

A presence nearby made his skin crawl, and he could sense—what? A finger, a hand, something else?—close to his face, but not touching. It hovered over him, the weight of it omnipresent as it made the flesh just above his cheekbone tingle, the fine hairs standing on end with a nervous warning.

He couldn't see it, couldn't tell what it was, but he sure as hell could *feel* it and knew that it was close. Very, very close. He could sense the scope of it, and it set all the alarms of his body ringing.

A warm breath washed across his face. The smell of it assaulted him, made him cough violently. It stank of rotting meat, but there was something else beneath—a musty stink, both fungal and fecal, an odor of old, wet, unwashed fabric, and a hemp-like scent that had trapped the funk of age. Briefly, Antoine was reminded of his grandmother's basement cedar closet and the rough, ancient fabrics that had been left to rot.

He choked on rising bile as he dug frantically for the knife in his pocket. He tried to lodge his thigh against the…the cocoon, he supposed—he refused to think of it as a coffin—to prevent the blade from slipping deeper down, but had no way of gauging his success.

That tingling itchy feeling in his face grew stronger and stronger, and then a bristle brushed against his cheek.

"Oh god," he gasped.

Why couldn't he reach that goddamn knife?

The susurration of that thing's breathing was loud in his ear, its exhalations hot on his skin. Rough hair poked into his face, scratching like steel wool. He wanted to see what was beside him, but at the same time, he was grateful that he couldn't.

He tried to jimmy the knife up with his middle finger, but his hands were slick with sweat. He was hot from his body heat trapped beneath this thick shell, his fried nerves, and the ever-growing fear as something loomed over and beside him in the dark.

Something hot and slick pushed against his ear. His skin felt raw where the tough, pointed hair of the creature had rubbed against him. A rough, wet weight slid across his cheek, up the side of his face. A fat, heavy drop of warm moisture slipped down his ear, pooling in the canal.

"Please stop," he muttered. "Please, just stop." His mind raced, cursing, and yes, even praising his sightlessness. He wanted to see what was before him, but he also very much did not want to see it. He was paralyzed by the cocoon as much as by fear.

The pain was immediate as his ear was ripped away from his skull, blood sheeting down his neck and leaking into the gap between his body and the shell that held him in place. His shirt and coat collar quickly grew sodden and sticky. Antoine's shrieks echoed all around him, until shock made the world fade away. When he woke again, he was disoriented. He had no idea how long he had been passed out for, but the memories flooded in on a fresh tide of panic.

Skittering sounds echoed around him, the noise so amplified by his blindness that it took him a moment to realize the noises were growing more distant.

Atop this was another noise, and it took him a moment to place the pathetic mewling as his own pained whimpers. He sounded like an injured dog, but he quickly realized he was alone. Whatever had attacked him had taken his ear as its prize and jittered away, leaving him to bleed.

Trapped, blinded, and in pain, a single terrifying thought circulated through his mind: *I'm going to die here. I don't even know where the fuck I am, and I'm going to die here.*

Tears burned beneath his glued-shut eyelids as a slick runner of snot fell across his upper lip. Panic gripped his heart in a vice and squeezed, choking loose another wet sob from deep within him.

I'm going to fucking die here, he thought again. And then, perversely, he thought of his boy's smile, of how Helix laughed in a moment of pure, unbridled joy over something so innocent, like the bulge of his father's cheek or the taste of a good, fresh grape.

No. No! Fuck that. Fuck! That! I ain't fucking dying here. No, no, no.

He strained his fingers as he reached for his pocket again, pulling the skin so taut he had the crazy image of flesh splitting to unsheathe the skeletal phalanges that would grab ahold of the knife in his pocket. He whined with the exertion, his heart racing so quickly the blood flow made a staccato beat inside his skull as a river of gore poured down the side of his face.

"Gah!" he screamed. "C'mon, Goddammit!"

His fingers strained and reached, his hand worming into the opposite hip pocket deep enough to pull on his shoulder, hard enough that he felt like the ball joint would pop right out of its socket, but still he reached—

And grabbed the smooth, pearl plated handle between his middle and forefinger. He held it in a tight curl, sweat popping up all along his forehead. He had to stomp on the panic and the urge to hurry. He knew he had to work fast, before that motherfucker came back for seconds, but he couldn't screw things up. He couldn't rush and risk losing the blade. He moved slowly and methodically, extracting his hand a fraction at a time.

God, how he wished he could see.

He got his hand free of the pocket, his forearm comfortably reseated against the shelf of the cocoon pressing against his belly. He hoped to hell he wasn't about to stab himself by accident.

His index finger found the release button, and the blade shot into place with a satisfying metallic snap. He allowed himself a glimmer of a smile, that simple flexion of muscles reminding him how woozy he felt from blood loss. Getting the knife had taken a lot out of him, more than he had anticipated. He couldn't pause and rest, though. There was no time for that.

He drew a deep breath to steady himself, then jabbed the blade forward as hard as he could. In such an enclosed space, and unable to generate much of a swing, it didn't do much. The sharp edge bit into the shell with a crunch, but he could tell it had not penetrated very far. He did what he could, though, delivering quick jabs to chip away at the tough surface boxing him in.

Finally, a noisy crack sounded, the noise rebounding off the rocky walls, and the blade pushed through. He twisted the blade in the small gap, working to make the hole big enough to get his fingers through. The pressure on his chest eased up a bit and he was able to push with his left arm.

A large piece of shell broke away and his aching lungs sucked in air as he elbowed away what he could. He felt lighter without the weight pressing on his torso. He folded the blade back into its handle and pocketed it, his hand going instantly to his eyes.

His fingers brushed against the rough coating over his face, feeling where the resin plastered over his eyes and dripped across his cheeks, covering the bridge of his nose. He worked his fingers under the edge of shell and pulled it away. His eyelids stretched as the cocoon broke away, tearing out his eyebrows and eyelashes, eliciting a brief, jagged cry.

I can see! Oh, god, thank fucking Christ, I can see.

As his eyes opened and adjusted to the dim, bluish-green light, he thought maybe seeing wasn't so great after all.

Antoine was glued into a nook at the corner of a wide cavern, close to the apex. He could hear chittering noises in the distance, the scraping of hard bristles on rock. All around him were more cocoons, and he could make out the mottled remains of those closest to him. A cropping of bioluminescent fungus clinging to the walls illuminated a corpse beside him, a thin layer of desiccated skin stretched tightly across bone. The face was missing its features—no ears, no nose. The lips were gone, leaving only a ragged flap of gray flesh hanging loosely over exposed teeth, and he couldn't tell if the person had been a man or a woman.

The corpse blinked, and Antoine yelped. He pulled manically at the shell covering his arm, then, once that arm was freed, began smacking and pulling at the coating over his legs and feet.

The mutilated form beside him turned, dead, blank eyes burning into his soul, and laughed. Its cackling grew louder, and soon, great peals of laughter came from the other shells around him. A cacophony of the crazed near-dead surrounded him, enshrouding him in the reverberations of their madness.

Antoine's heart pummeled his ribs, threatening to burst free of its cage. With his legs free, he held himself close to the wall, gripping the rough stone with all his strength. His muscles burned, and he tried to figure out how to make his descent. He figured he was about fifty feet up, too far to simply drop to the ground. *That's all I need,* he thought. *Get me some broken legs, some shattered ankles. Yeah, that'd be real good.*

Laughter echoed in the cavern, rattling his already ruined nerves. He adjusted himself with an utter lack of finesse to face the rock wall and slowly, nervously, lowered himself. The wall was crowded with the sacks of victims, and each one that he passed stared at him with insane eyes too large for the hollows they inhabited. He turned his gaze away from the sunken faces and toothless, ancient mouths of these papyrus abominations. He had to get away before their madness engulfed him as well.

Grime from the walls coated his slick hands like rosin, helping him get a better grip on whatever hand and footholds he managed to find.

He had just carefully landed on a small shelf of rock, the ledge barely wide enough to press the tips of his shoes onto, when it collapsed beneath him. The scree of rock and loose soil clattered down the wall and he fell with it, trying to grab onto something, anything. The nails on his right hand tore out of their beds and he hollered, reaching for whatever he could.

His left hand snagged a handful of thin hair, his weight snapping the neck of a cocooned victim. He, or she, had tried to scream in its final moments and he caught a whiff of gassy breath, a repulsive stench of death. The skin of the corpse was so thin, its body so emaciated, that the head broke free of the spinal column and Antoine found himself falling once again, this time with a stranger's head in hand.

He landed atop another cocoon, grabbing it around the shoulder area and straddling it. Repulsed, he dropped the severed head and stared at the gaunt face of the person beneath him.

"Help," it moaned, voice cracking with brittle dryness, its breath tepid and awful in his face.

Antoine wanted to help, wanted to tell this person that he would…that he would if he could, and explain that he didn't know how to right now. He would bring back help, though. He wanted to tell this person not to worry, that he would send help as soon as he could.

Instead, he said nothing and maneuvered across the shell. The rough material left his hand raw as he made his way back to the wall. He couldn't climb over any more of these people, these dead or dying souls, and the madness they'd lost themselves to. He couldn't.

He was close to the bottom, close enough to drop down. His knees buckled in exhaustion as soon as his feet hit solid ground, and he collapsed in a heap. He laid still for a moment, working to catch his breath even as waves of nausea slammed against him. His fingers were bloody, the pain at the side of his head unlike anything he had ever felt before.

Ahead, he could make out a darker shape in this dimly lit cavern. Slowly approaching it, he could discern that the darker recess was a tunnel carved into the earth. He didn't see any other points of entry into the cavern, and above was only a domed ceiling bouncing crazed howls and laughter from above back down to him.

He looked for a weapon, but there was little of use. He had the knife in his pocket, and he took it out again, flicking the blade into place, but he needed something more. Searching the ground, he found a rock of suitable size and tested its heft. The weight was good, and it nice and solid. It might not do a lot of damage, but it would, perhaps, make something think twice after a good crack on the skull.

His whole body a blister of pain, he slowly, and with a degree of hesitation, made his way down the tunnel toward the skittering sounds of scritching and scratching.

FIVE

A HAND TORE FREE from the wall and grabbed Antoine's bicep before he could make it to the opening.

"Stop, please, stop. You have to help me." The words came out in a dry, croaking rasp.

Turning, he met the first set of sane eyes he had seen in his time here. The face was gaunt, the skin dusky, but the man clearly still had life in him. Not much, perhaps, but enough—and certainly far more than the others Antoine had witnessed.

Antoine had deserted the last figure to plead for his help. Now that he was on solid ground and face-to-face with somebody possessing a measure of vitality, he found it harder to ignore and began chiseling at the cocoon with his knife.

"You have to get me out of here. Hurry, hurry, hurry."

"Man, I'm going as fast as I can."

Noises echoed down the tunnel, their approach rapid.

"Come on, hurry!" The poor wretch was sobbing, his begging voice hitching in his throat as he choked on his tears.

"Man, shut up. You're attracting them here. Shut up!"

The man cried louder, screaming, "Help! Help me!"

Antoine couldn't keep his anger, nor his panic, at bay. It overwhelmed him as the man loudly insisted on rushing him. He reared back one arm and delivered a swift punch, shattering the guy's nose. He hit him a second time, and then a third, the stranger's teeth cutting Antoine's knuckles.

Hairy limbs scrabbled across rock, along with another sound that sent a primal shiver of fear through Antoine's spine. The noise shifted between shrill squeaking and guttural snorts, an awful and inhuman line of communication that was impossible to decipher, but which nonetheless frightened him terribly.

The man continued to howl hysterically, "Geb me out, geb me out, geb me out!" Flecks of blood flew from his mouth as crimson sheeted over his lips and chin.

Antoine cracked the shell and pulled as hard as he could. A hard chunk of resin came loose and he very nearly fell on his ass. He tossed the broken material aside and resumed his work, getting the man's arm free.

"Help me out of here," Antoine said, encouragingly. "C'mon, I need your help."

In the dim fungal glow, the shadows shifted deeper in the cavern as a pale creature moved through the murk, drawing nearer.

And then it was upon them.

"Oh no, no, no, no, no," the man screamed. His legs were still entombed, and he waved his arms as the creature stormed toward him.

Antoine stood stock still, paralyzed with shock and fear.

Although the creature was alone, its alien presence was enough to intimidate, and Antoine's mind struggled to identify and label it. A monster? A bug? He had no idea how to classify it, knowing only that it was large and repulsive. The thing was all sharp edges and thorns, and it stood roughly hip-high on a trio of spikey legs. Pointed fur stood in violent patches, revealing alabaster skin beneath. Clusters of milky red, spidery eyes watched him, even as its forelimbs reached toward the emaciated man shrinking against the wall and flapping his arms, as if he could shoo the beast away.

Antoine shoved himself away from the broken cocoon and pressed against the opposite wall, enthralled by the display. A series of mandibles unfolded from the creature's trapezoidal head, and long, hairy flaps unfurling from a pink, striated mass of flesh to reveal a toothy maw. A nature show that Antoine occasionally watched had once featured leatherback turtles, and he recalled the repulsive image of the inside of that turtle's mouth, seeing it again here in this odd monstrosity's maw. A gaping hole filled with rows upon rows of barbed teeth lined the entirety of the thing's orifice, and all down its throat. It turned to the screaming man, its arm lashing out lightning-quick and gripping his face in three, long fingers that ended in daggers.

Although the monster had turned away from Antoine, he still saw a tongue-like spike dart out of its mouth. The barbs dug into the man's skin, and the beast licked upward, stripping the flesh off that side of his face. The man's screams grew louder, more panicked, as he thrashed, and Antoine caught a glimpse of a nightmare as ragged skin gave way to raw muscle and flashes of bone. He wondered if that was he how he had lost his ear, and if this thing was responsible. Still, he was rooted to the earth, his legs frozen tubes of lead, unable to move.

The creature strode up the wall, still holding the man's face in its slender hands, turning the head at an unnatural angle as it crawled, positioning itself above the man and twisting the skull savagely between its forelimbs. There was sharp crack of a shattering spine, and then the beast let go. The man's head flopped uselessly, hanging limply from a twisted knot of bone jutting awkwardly beneath the flesh of his neck. Its pointed toes clicked on the rock, lowering itself further, and grasped the head again. The muscular flaps covering its mouth wrapped over the man's pate, and then there was a bony cracking noise followed by an awful slurping sound.

Piss ran down Antoine's leg, the acrid scent drawing the creature's attention.

A chittering noise burst from the beast as its legs carried it down the wall, using the man's torso as a springboard to leap forward. It smacked into Antoine, toppling him to the ground and standing on his chest. It reared back, extending its long, slender arms forward and snapping its long digits toward Antoine's face like scissors. Pinned to the ground, Antoine saw a long, slender stalk swinging from between the creature's arrangement of legs.

So, you're a boy, huh? he thought, nearly driven to laughter by the madness of the sudden thought. Crazed laughter exploded loose as he realized he still held the knife, even as his free hand searched the ground for another weapon. His fingers grazed a good-sized chunk of resin he had cracked away from the dead man's cocoon and grabbed ahold of it, acting fast and without much thought.

Antoine socked the monster in the side of its massive head with the large fragment of shell. The beast was momentarily dazed, then quickly shook off the blow. Its face unfolded and, once again, Antoine was staring down that black cavern of teeth, close enough to see the small barbs and lances serrating the surface of each prong. It hissed at him, a fresh coppery scent on its breath.

He swung the shell again, but the creature raised an arm to block the blow. It deflected him easily, surprising Antoine with its muscular strength. While the monster was distracted by this feint, he jabbed the knife forward, into what he presumed was the beast's belly.

Brackish green ichor spilled over his hands. Shrill screaming pierced his ear, like tenterhooks snagging his brain and yanking at the gray matter insistently. Strong forelimbs batted at his face, one of the claws drawing a wending tract across his face. Antoine twisted the knife, savagely tearing it free and then stabbing the creature again, and again, and again. The stench was foul, briny, and alkaline, the monster's blood washing over him and making his exposed skin itch madly.

As the monster thrashed, its forelimbs swung at him, the pointy ends of its praying mantis-like arms stabbing into Antoine's chest and shoulder. He did what he could to avoid the blows, but on his back and confined beneath the disgusting thing, he had too little room to maneuver. He continued his assault, his arm wearing out quickly as already fatigued muscles burned in protest. The ichor burned his nose as he inhaled its stink, and before long the monster lost its fight. It slowed and sank down against him, its life force spilling out all around them, and then it was dead.

Antoine shoved his way out from beneath the creature and shot to his feet. He wanted to shake off the gore in a nervous, limb-flapping dance of shivery disgust, but he couldn't summon the energy. Instead, he flicked his arms out, splattering the walls on either side with gore, knowing he would not get much cleaner than this. Not until he was out this damn hole.

Where the fuck am I?

The salesman had led him to an office in the back of the showroom, but his memories after that were a blur. He recalled a sting and then falling down a long stretch of stairs. Was this beneath the dealership?

He shook his head, wondering what the hell had happened, and how he had gone from maybe collecting five large to this. The course of events was so unnatural, so *alien*, that he struggled to accept how Point A led to Point B. A wild nightmare of a Point B, no less. He had no idea how far down he was, or where he was, or how he had gotten into this cavern…although he figured beneath the car dealership was a good-enough guess and probably the most likely.

The monsters must have brought him here, he decided, after he had tumbled down the stairs. They had dragged him and strung him up in some kind of cocoon, leaving him to rot and snack on. The side of his head ached from where his ear had once been, in concert with the hot stinging from the shallow trench that had been carved down his mug.

That salesman—he'd never gotten his name—had to know about this. The fucker had stabbed him in the neck, injected him with some kind of drug that had made him woozy as fuck. When he had turned to look at the chubby salesman, he saw that fat face grinning at him, holding up a needle. Whatever had been inside that syringe worked quickly. Antoine had taken a reflexive step backward and lost his footing. The pain of hitting those rocky steps had been the only thing preventing him from passing out so quickly, but once he had hit the bottom, it was lights out.

I told you it was a fucking scam, Channy!

Oh Channy, baby…

He remembered his phone and thrust his hand into the pocket of his sodden carpenter's coat. It was still there! Apparently dumping him down the stairs had been good enough for that son of a bitch. Nobody had bothered to search Antoine for any personal effects. He breathed a sigh of relief as he took the phone out.

Then he saw the shattered case. The old cell phone had been reduced to a flimsy collection of plastic shards barely held together by faint luck. He risked opening it, but, as he suspected, the screen stayed dark. He imagined between rolling down the steps and fighting with that fucking overgrown cockroach that had been all she wrote on the phone.

Shadows shifted in the tunnel, and he wondered if more of those things were coming his way. Their noises did not seem any closer, and he wondered if his eyes were simply playing tricks on him.

He looked at the bug-monster thing, its white flesh unnaturally pale. He'd never seen anything even remotely like that. Hell, he had never even *heard* of anything like that. In high school, he'd had anatomy classes that did dissections every year, at least until the budget got cut and then dried up completely, and that part of their curriculum was slashed. He had dissected a worm and a frog before, and his books had images of other bugs and their gross anatomy—usually buried under scores of graffiti and crudely drawn dick pics. Later, in college, he had decided to major in biology and did a few more dissections in labs, at least until his arrest tanked his GPA and cost him his scholarship. Nothing in those courses was comparable to the thing at his feet. He liked watching documentaries, and sometimes PBS aired ones about the Earth's various lifeforms and ecologies, but nothing that was even remotely similar to the creature at his feet. This bug was a total unknown to him.

Fucker had been hard to kill, too. And it was big, bigger than any kind of insect Antoine had ever seen. Damn thing wasn't a housefly or simple little spider, that much was for sure. Even though it was roughly half the size of Antoine, it had been strong. Heavy, too. The flesh over its belly was thick and muscular, and covered with chitinous plating. From between these plates, long spikes of hair jutted forth. Perversely, Antoine was reminded of weeds growing between cracks in the sidewalk outside his apartment building.

Absently, he scratched at his face. The relief was immediate, but short-lived. Everywhere the creature's blood had touched felt hot and itchy, as if he had rubbed against poison ivy. He tried to ignore it, but the itching added another layer of discomfort to his misery. His face felt puffy as well, and the winding gouge the beast had clawed across his nose and cheeks inflamed and achy.

An unsettling quiet blanketed the cavern in the wake of the creature's death. The insane laughter of all those desiccated, barely alive bodies above had dwindled into silence, and Antoine felt hyper-aware of the skittering noises at the opposite end of the tunnel.

He dreaded passing through the small adit, but there were no other alternatives. He could not stay under this dome of rock, home to the dead and dying, cocooned all around him to the walls and ceiling. He had to move forward.

The shaft had clearly been burrowed by the creatures and was barely larger than the monster he had killed. Getting down on hands and knees, his crawled into the entryway, the hole's rough ceiling little more than a finger's width above his head.

Antoine had never considered himself claustrophobic, but the shadowy, confining space so soon after he had freed himself from the hard shell that had engulfed him sent a surge of panic rising through him. He had to stop and force himself to regulate his breathing. Then he decided to flatten himself to the floor and put more distance between his body and the tunnel's low ceiling, thinking he would have an easier time of it if he army crawled his way through.

He had to get to the other side of this tunnel. He had to see Channy and Helix again, and tell them how much he loved them both. Guilt racked him as he thought about leaving the apartment in angry frustration. The kid's screaming had worn on his nerves, and he knew trying to collect money from the car dealership was a wild goose chase. He also knew that Channy would just keep harping on him, picking away at his resolve, until he caved and agreed to follow her advice.

There had been a time when Antoine had considered leaving both Channy and Helix. Back when he had a job, at least. Somedays, Channy could be too much to bear. And then there was the baby…besides all those diapers, the constant need for attention that ate up all his time and energy, the screaming and crying. Dealing with Channy by herself was a handful, but add in a kid? Nah, no thanks, he'd thought. Better to just pack up, find somewhere to lay his head, and keep whatever money he earned fixing up cars. Let Channy go out and get a job, feel what it was like to support herself and baby for a time.

Then, almost as soon as those thoughts appeared, another rush of feelings followed—guilt, a sadness so strong it reduced him to a sobbing wreck, and a resolve to be better and stronger. Because the truth of it was, despite how overwhelming his home life was, he honestly did love his girl and his baby boy. And he was going to get back to them.

His arms and legs slid across the ground, moving him closer to the opening at the opposite end of the tunnel and further away from that nightmarish cavern he had awoken in. The side of his head itched, burning where dirt rubbed into the open wound where his ear had been. Ignoring the pain, he thought of his family, his light at the end of all this. He missed the weight of Helix in his arms, the boy's tiny body pressed to his chest. That weight gave Antoine comfort, gave his love for the child a certain solidity, and what he needed more than anything else at that moment was to hold Helix once more. He wanted to wrap the child tightly in his arms and smother him with kisses, to feel the boy's slobbery lips against his own as he speckled the child's face with fatherly affection. He imagined Helix would spend those moments grabbing his nose or cheeks, as he had done so often before. That memory was so strong, Antoine could not help but smile…and that smile nearly broken him. Even after all he had seen over the course of this evening, the fact he could still smile was astounding.

"I miss you so much right now, Helix." He whispered the words into his forearm, momentarily resting his head to sooth his aching neck. "Daddy's coming home."

He resumed crawling, inching his way through the shaft. The closer he got to the end of this tunnel, he told himself, the closer he would be to his family. He swore to himself that he would do better by Channy and Helix. The first thing he was going to do once he stepped foot back in their apartment was wrap his girl in his arms and kiss her, long and hard, like he hadn't in...too long, he realized. Far too long.

"She'll probably be in her robe," he said, chuckling softly. She had this big, fluffy green robe, soft as all get out, and she loved wearing it. If she could, she'd live in that damn robe, that was how much she loved it. He was going to hold her close, maybe slip his hands inside the garment, rest his palms on her pajama-clad hips. Her bedroom attire wasn't exactly Frederick's of Hollywood these days, and he figured most men wouldn't find a giant fleece robe all that sexy, but thinking of her now, all that was very, very appealing. In many ways, it was sexy *because* it wasn't fancy. He needed to tell her how much he loved her, let her know everything was going to be okay. He was going to find another job, set things right again, get everything back on track. First, though, he just needed to hold onto her a little bit, let that reassuring warmth of her body radiate over him.

Maybe in holding his girl and his son, he could start putting the pieces of himself back together.

He just needed to get home.

The tunnel began to widen near the opening. An odd silence hung in the air. He couldn't help but wonder where the bugs were and why they weren't making their customary racket. He'd been hearing them chittering and scampering about for so long, the quiet that had settled in was disturbing.

He paused a foot shy of the opening, trying to look into the space beyond. He couldn't see much. The bottom edges of more cocoons, but little else. He tried, and failed, not to think about the bugs scaling the walls and that maybe they were looming overhead, waiting for him to stick his head out of the hole and pounce. A terrifying image of himself coming half out of the tunnel invaded his head, and he could practically feel the crunch as the back of his skull exploded in one of those creature's mouths. He shook the image away.

No sense scaring yourself now, he thought.

After giving it another minute, he decided to move forward. Not that he had any other choice, he knew. There was only one way out, and it was not behind him.

The air felt cooler on his skin as he stood. He was hot and sweaty, so the temperature change was not significantly different, but nonetheless welcome. He swiped the moisture away from his face with his forearm and studied this new chamber.

As with the previous cavern, he found himself in a rocky dome filled clusters of mushrooms that emitted a gentle green glow and revealed a number of cocoons along the walls. His stomach lurched at the sight. Some cocoons were cracked apart, leaving broken shells clinging to the walls around him, but several held bodies that were barely recognizable as human in their current condition, lost somewhere between near-death and decay. What little of their forms was exposed was emaciated and riddled with sores.

A cocooned woman canted her head to look at him with unfocused eyes. She opened her mouth to reveal only a black pit. Her teeth had fallen out, or perhaps had been ripped out, he thought, noticing that her tongue was missing as well.

She wheezed at him, and he was grateful not to be close enough to smell her breath. The skin of her throat shifted, a misshapen bulge rising in her thin, skeletal neck. She gagged, choking for what seemed an impossibly long time. Her face jutted toward his, and he stepped back as her eyes widened with panic.

Her mouth stretched wider, the tendons in her jaw snapping as something climbed up the back of her throat. Thin, pointed, white fingers gripped either side of her dry, cracked, and painfully parted lips as it birthed itself from her mouth.

SIX

THE FIRST THING JON Dangle did each morning was check the integrity of what his ancestors had called a Sipapu, or, as he called it, the Vault. Unlocking the white door, he peeked his head in and saw that the trap door to the stairs was fastened securely. Then, he walked over and gave the padlock a good tug, satisfied that it still held.

He relocked the white door behind him and headed into the monitoring room across the hall. The screens, as always, were on. His brother, Jensen, was not in yet, but that was not unusual. Dangle had always been an early riser, and he liked being the first person into work, liked making that first pot of coffee and inhaling the aroma of the grounds as they brewed.

Pointing his attention to one specific screen, broadcasting the live-feed from down below, he saw that DeWitt's body was gone, as expected. Surveillance cameras were mounted in the Vault, one on either of side of the door separating the roughly carved steps from the chamber beyond. No other cameras were installed beyond that door. An attempt had been made, once, to wire the tunnel leading to the colony, but after his father had been mauled, and was somehow lucky enough to escape, they had never tried again. Dangle presumed it was for the best. He did not want to see what those creatures did to their food, or whatever else they did down there all day. There were no lights in the Vault, nor in the tunnel, so the cameras recorded on night-vision mode.

Less than twelve hours had passed since he had injected DeWitt with Dilaudid, an opioid he was able to order in liquid form from a connection he had established on the dark net. The drug was fast acting, and he hoped that the painkiller helped ease the suffering for which he was partly responsible. Of course, falling down the stairs had probably helped DeWitt lose consciousness. The large man had taken quite a nasty fall.

Dangle queued up last night's recording, and rewound through nearly twelve hours of static imagery of the empty vault until he landed on a flash of movement that was all too familiar. On screen, DeWitt crashed into the ground, his eyes unfocused as they rolled up into the back of his skull, his head slumping to the side as he went unconscious. A few minutes later, Dangle recognized his own feet coming down the steps and then he walked into view.

Christ, am I really that fat? he thought, seeing himself on screen. The camera added ten pounds, but he had certainly added plenty more all by himself. He had been surprised six months ago when he saw his bulky frame on screen, larger than he'd remembered it being just a few months prior. Now, he looked downright obese. *I gotta work on that.*

Once, Dangle had been a health nut. All through his teens and twenties, he had eaten well and exercised at least an hour every day, alternating between weightlifting and cardio. He had looked good, strong and chiseled, a nice set of muscles on his arms and chest, with a flat stomach. He had felt good, too. He'd been able to score plenty of women, and pussy had been a solid motivator to keep him at the gym. Until he found himself in a relationship…

Marla was a fine wife. Much of their early courtship had been spent in the bedroom, their relationship spurred on by mutual lust that turned into love as they learned more about one another. She was a homebody, though, and enjoyed spending nights inside to read or watch TV. She had a nice, natural figure, curves he could eye all day, and he certainly didn't mind staying indoors with her. As his attention turned toward her more and more often, he found himself growing into a sedentary lifestyle. Marla was also a wonderful cook, and as their passions cooled they found themselves often occupied by television and a warm plate of food.

Dangle had not initially been bothered by the weight he had put on as the first year of their relationship turned into a second, and he always thought he could lose it quickly. He found, though, that quitting the gym had been too easy—much easier than going back to it. Ten years later, he was wearing pants six sizes larger and his weight was about sixty pounds heavier. Marla, too, had put on her share of pounds, and her apple bottom had thickened and spread, until the rest of her was apple, and then orange-shaped, as well.

Maybe it was time to start working out again. He was a few years shy of forty, still plenty of time to turn this ship around.

He doubted he would be able to get his body back in the shape it had been a decade ago, but he could at least get his weight down, maybe even get to be solid looking again, have a body more like DeWitt's. DeWitt had been thick, but Dangle had felt the thick slabs of muscle under the man's bulky coat.

Dangle watched on the split-screen as DeWitt's feet vanished through the door as Dangle dragged him deep enough into the tunnel to clear the door's arc.

The cameras were video only, so sitting in the monitoring room, Dangle couldn't hear the scratching noises the bugs made as they sensed, and then were drawn to, the fresh meat. He was grateful to be saved from that noise a second time; just imagining it was enough to raise the hair on his arms.

Onscreen, he stepped over DeWitt's prone form, pulling the door shut behind him. On one half of the monitor, Dangle climbed up the stairs, while on the other half, DeWitt laid perfectly still.

Nothing happened for a long stretch of time, and Dangle sped through nearly an hour of footage. He knew DeWitt could not have gotten free, but he had to be sure. He had to see it.

A flicker of movement at the edge of the screen caught his attention, and he thought he could see the hint of a sharp-clawed leg. The creature's skin was a stark white against the green glow of the camera's night vision. Slowly, it came forward, its head angling at an awkward angle to observe DeWitt. It circled his body, cocking its head in curiosity, and then leaned in close to smell him. After a few good sniffs, it reared back and raised its face to the ceiling, its mouth opening.

Again, Dangle was grateful he could not hear the vocalizations coming from that creature's undulating throat. He had seen this display often enough to know that it was signaling for help. Sure enough, several more of the creatures came into view and situated themselves around DeWitt. In unison, they grabbed his arms and legs and, hoisting him overhead, began carrying him down the tunnel, like ants carrying away stolen goods from a picnic.

Satisfied, Dangle turned off the recording. His stomach grumbled, and his eyes were still heavy with sleep. He needed coffee. And maybe one or two of those chocolate biscotti tucked away in the cupboards.

SEVEN

DIGITS CLAMPED ON EITHER side of the woman's mouth, her scream a garbled, suffocated plea as the monster shimmied its way up her throat. As the thing worked its way up, its arms and head forced her orifice wider. Her lips stretched, the skin blanching under the strain, and then the corners of her mouth split, the flesh unzipping into a gruesome and jagged smile as her cheeks ripped apart. A noise like that of an elastic band snapping was followed by a loud crunch as her jaw dislocated and hung flimsily from the broken struts of her face.

Antoine was stuck in place, his brain struggling to process what his eyes were seeing. And the woman...! Oh, Jesus. Jesus Christ, the woman was still alive. Trapped, in pain, but still alive. Her screams were muffled by the gargle of blood and the body of so foreign an object wetly slinking its way free. The white skin of the creature was slick with a skein of gore, and Antoine swore he could hear the hairs on its body scraping against the roof of the woman's mouth.

He had to get out of here.

He turned, but the sound of crackling forced him to look back.

A pointed arm burst through the cocoon, caked in gore. Shredded strings of entrails hung from the end of its dagger-like limbs, and the woman hollered in that painfully muted, clogged way. More limbs jutted from her, exploding free of her torso and punching out of the shell.

The creature in her mouth, its head crowned between her broken, mutilated lips, turned toward the ceiling. Its serrated arms dug into either side of the upper part of her head as it pulled free of her oral cavity, squirming its way loose.

Once it had finally dislodged itself, the woman's head lifelessly slumped forward. It crawled up her face, into the thin gray strands of hair speckling her scalp. The other creatures, dozens of them, all smaller than the mouth breacher, wormed out of the cavity in her torso and through the broken shell, climbing up her to join the larger bug nesting in the remains of her hair.

The front of the cocoon had burst apart, and Antoine stared at the hollowed remains of her torso. Bile rose in his throat, and he choked on it as his stomach spasmed painfully enough that he wished he had something inside him to vomit. His knees nearly buckled, his hand shooting out to catch the wall beside him. His arms and legs shook with a sudden weak exhaustion.

He wretched and gagged, dry heaving, spitting out the moisture his salivary glands flooded his mouth with. Part of him knew he was making far too much noise, and another part cared not at all.

A tapping noise echoed in the chamber, prompting him to look at the woman's remains. The bugs were climbing the wall and traveling in a narrow line toward him, like ants on the march.

Click. Click. Click.

From behind, he heard more crackling noises and the sound of shells breaking. He turned in time to see multiple bodies rupture, dozens more of these strange creatures hurtling out of the wrecked remains. A skittering flood of pale white bodies shifting and shimmering rushed toward him. It sounded like the popping of bubble wrap.

Wracked by indecision, he looked back at the tunnel he had come through. It was the only way out.

And that goes right into another dead end, he thought.

He had nowhere to run to, no place to hide.

He was too slow, anyway.

As he turned to move toward the tunnel, one freshly hatched bug leapt off the wall and slammed into him, the points of its legs and arms cutting into his flesh and hooking into his muscles. He ripped it away with a scream and slammed it into a wall. Its face turned into a lumpy mush as it fell lifelessly to the floor. The others were on him, a handful at first, and then more.

Antoine dropped and rolled on the ground. The bugs, still young and small, made plaintive clicking sounds as he crushed them beneath his body. The fine, sharp ends of their hair pricked his skin through his shirt and jeans. Hooked limbs stabbed at him, poking holes in his chest and face and neck, his arms and legs. He moaned, his body itching and burning and bleeding. His heels kicked at the ground, moving him closer to the tunnel. A swarm rushed up his legs and he jolted to his feet, shaking his limbs, hoping he could fling them off. They were stuck to him, though. He stepped on what he could, smashing their bodies beneath his boots, brushing off more with violent sweeps of his hands.

He bumped into a wet, mushy mess and turned. His eyes met the empty glare of the dead woman, and he stumbled back. More of the shell crumbled away on contact and the woman slumped forward, as if following him. One arm hung loose, the bones visible beneath thin, sickly translucent skin.

"God forgive me," he said.

He grabbed her arm and pulled. The shell broke away as she tumbled out of it and fell to the ground. He planted a boot on her back, disgusted with what he was about to do. Beneath her ruined shirt, her body sank much too deeply beneath his heel, as if her flesh was little more than jelly.

"Oh God, forgive me," he said again, then twisted and savagely pulled at her arm. Wet, paper-like skin slipped loose from the bones in his hands, cartilage creaking and snapping, flesh shredding away from the shoulder with an awful tear as he pulled the arm free from its socket.

He swung the arm out at the oncoming horde of bugs, slamming the rounded head of the humerus into a handful and sweeping them aside. More were crawling up his flanks and he swiped at them with his free hand, jabbing the bone at the others. He swung, smashing the bugs on the wall, then swept away more of them onto the ground. One leapt at him, and he caught it just right, swinging at it and knocking it into the wall with a wet thud. He stomped on those that drew near.

Blood leaked down his back, and pinpricks of pain ran up his spine to his neck, stabbing into his shoulders. He backed into the wall, hard, practically throwing himself against the rocky earth. He grinned like a maniac as their bodies smashed apart beneath him.

He ran the bone down the length of his chest and legs, sweeping the bugs away from him. He kicked and stepped on them as they landed.

Panting, he stood there, gripping the woman's severed arm in both hands and holding it before him, waiting, listening. His whole body burned, the pain made worse by all of the aggravated itchiness.

The cavern was silent, save for his rapid, noisy breathing. On each inhalation, he caught the acrid stink of the ichor coating him, mingling with the earthy rot around him and the putrid stench of his own fear.

He had to go on, had to continue ahead into the chamber beyond.

He had to get home.

EIGHT

DANGLE FED THE MONEY Carlo flyer to the shredder, listening to the machine grind away and watching as Antoine DeWitt's name and address slid into the chomping metal maw of swirling teeth. He should have destroyed it last night, but he had gotten lazy.

Laziness was no excuse. He could practically hear his father reminding him that this dealership had not stayed in business over three generations due to laziness. That the Ba'is living beneath it had not stayed hidden because of their family's laziness. That no evidence leading to those that were abducted and disappeared into the tunnels below had led to their arrests was not due to a stockpile of laziness, but because of due diligence entirely. No, Jon Dangle, his father would remind him, their family had not come this far and succeeded for this long because they were lazy.

So get your fucking shit together, and get your ass in gear, you stupid son of a bitch. How many times had he heard his father say that last bit? Often enough that it was practically dear old dad's catchphrase. More often that Dangle cared to admit, which was much too often indeed. Or, as his father would have said, one time too many.

Like those that had come before him, Jon Dangle worked hard at keeping the Ba'is a secret. And, like his ancestors before him, he was not always as successful as he would have liked. While rare, it happened on occasion that one or two of the beasts got loose by burrowing their way aboveground. Usually it was out in the woods, and maybe a naturalist or hiker wandering through caught sight of the unusual creature…or went missing altogether. By no means was this a regular occurrence, but every now and then Dangle heard rumors, or suggestions of an urban legend about what was out in the woods. Sometimes, a customer would ask and Dangle would just scoff.

"You don't actually believe that, do you?" he'd say, and nine out of ten times the conversation would end right then and there. If the customer persisted, Dangle would educate them on the legend, explaining it as a heavily exaggerated holdover from Potawatomi stories about the mischievous nature spirits they called Ba'is. These stories were influenced, if not outright cannibalized, by other Native American legends and stories, and creation myths shared from tribe to tribe and embellished by time. The Mandan, for instance, spoke of their ancestors as having emerged from subterranean lands through caves along the Missouri River. Apache and Iroquois tribes told similar tales, and the Hopi spoke of a Sipapu entrance in the Grand Canyon that led to the underworld. This Sipapu was not unlike the Vault Dangle's people had watched over and protected for centuries, and, according to Hopi Sacred Stories, it was from a Sipapu that the first people emerged. Those first people were lizard-like creatures that morphed into human form and began to settle the sun-kissed land. Although he was many generations removed from his Native American ancestors who had first settled the area and found a way to tame and care for the creatures below, he knew enough about their history and lore to tell a convincing and entertaining story.

When it came time to feed the Ba'is, the Dangle clan had always been careful. No locals, and keep the victims differentiated as best as you can. Don't only take blacks or whites or redheads, never draw too often or too quickly from the same towns or regions, and, when using the Money Carlo scam, cast the net wide and don't send the ticket to the same address more than once every few years.

Occasionally, he or Jensen would take out one of the fleet vans and snatch a hobo. That was usually the safest bet and kept the Ba'is in good supply for a while. Nobody missed a bum.

It helped, too, that the dealership was situated well past the outskirts of the sleepy little village. The police department was small, and Dangle regularly contributed a healthy amount to their annual fundraisers. He also donated to the city council's incumbents, which gave him an extra layer of coverage if he ever needed to pull in favors. For the most part, the police were interested in issuing speeding tickets and little else, unless pressed into service. They did not go looking for trouble, for the simple fact that little in the way of trouble ever happened around here. If anything, it was the town's quietude that gave rise to such urban legends during those odd moments, once or twice a decade, when a local did disappear, or somebody thought they saw something unusual and whispered about it in a bar to a confidant or on a pillow beside a lover. Such rumors were a way to spice up an otherwise staid existence. Nobody *wanted* murders or abductions, but the stories gave them an entertaining outlet to stoke and stave their worries upon.

Antoine DeWitt would be missed by no one. If police ever did make it as far as this dealership in their search, presuming they were enlisted to search for him at all, Dangle would be open and honest. *Well, yes, officer, he did come here. He was interested in a new vehicle, and we ran a credit report on him. We weren't able to give him what he wanted, and he left. He walked right back out and that was the last I saw of him.*

He unwrapped a third biscotti and drowned it in coffee as the shredder beneath his desk spun to a halt.

Twenty years he'd been working at the dealership, first under his grandfather, and then his father. At seventeen, he had been brought into the fold and told about the cellar and what lurked below. He was a few years older than his brother, and Jensen had been spared the worst of the initiation.

Whereas Dangle was into lifting weights and chasing girls, his brother had been meek, more prone to playing computer games or watching movies and obsessing over their childhood home's audio-visual components. Jensen was spared ever getting his hands dirty, his status as the family's baby ever persistent. At first, Dangle had been jealous that his younger brother's innocence was allowed to remain intact. A gulf blossomed between the siblings, exacerbated by Jensen's natural introversion, and remained even after Jensen had been similarly introduced to the secret half of their family's business.

A few days after turning seventeen, Dangle had gone on his first ride along with his father, luring a white homeless man to their van with a roast beef sandwich. His father had clubbed the beggar over the head, and Dangle hauled the filthy, stinking vagrant into the van through the windowless sliding panel door. An hour later, they were rolling the bum down the stairs and into the tunnel's opening.

"What are they?" he had asked.

"Don't know, exactly." His father had told him the tribal stories of the Ba'is, and Dangle had listened attentively, absorbing it all. Memorizing every word the old man passed down to him.

"Where did they come from?"

"Don't know."

"Do they ever get out?"

At that, his father paused for a while, as if considering. He had been working on a cigarette, and he filled the silence with a long drag and a slow exhalation of smoke. "Sometimes," he finally admitted. "Not often, though. Not if we keep them fed. We keep them fed, they got no reason to go looking for food and they don't get out."

"So we keep them fed."

His father nodded. "We keep them fed."

It had been that way for generations, back when the surrounding lands had been little more than woods and farmland, and presumably long before then, as well, before even the Potawatomi had settled the region, long before the white men came. Time and mortal memory had a way of making history fuzzy, but the Ba'is remained.

Dangle thought of his family as guardians, watchers. Gatekeepers. They kept the Ba'is underground, which kept people safe. And like any necessary and valuable job, it occasionally required blood and sacrifice.

The biscotti was so drenched in coffee that when he laid it on his tongue, it slipped apart on contact, dissolving into wet chunks. It was delicious.

NINE

ANTOINE HAD NEVER WANTED to go home so badly. Too often, he'd felt the opposite and home was the last place he wanted to be. The number of times he thought about going elsewhere, of just leaving with whatever clothes he had on his back and disappearing into the night, was too high to count. Although he always went home at the end of the day, each time it was with a measure of regret. He would approach his apartment door knowing it was only a matter of time before he left Channy and Helix, and maybe after he was out of both of their lives, the weight he carried would lift from his bowed shoulders.

Most nights, he came home to a crying baby, Channy just sitting there, smoking. She would tell him, before he even had the door closed and locked behind him, before he even had a chance to get his shoes off, "You need to empty the dishwasher. There's laundry needs doing, too."

She would sit there, arms folded across her chest, a cigarette pinched between her fingers. Telling him what needed doing and that he needed to do it. As if he weren't the one working and bringing in the money, and still having nothing at all to show for it. As if he'd been the one home all day long, smoking like a chimney and doing fuck all else.

Yeah, I need to do all that, he'd think. Maybe he was pussy whipped, or maybe he had simply gotten too comfortable being under her thumb...and she had certainly gotten awfully comfortable keeping that thumb pressed down on him, that was for sure. However, he also knew that if he did not do those things, they wouldn't get done at all. Dishes would pile up, and the floor would be covered in dirty clothes.

On those rare nights when he had the energy to argue, they'd fight. They'd accuse each other and drum up makeshift lists of who did what to try to prove who was the real contributor at the home front, and, later, after the blood rage had died down, they'd both promise to do better and be better. Nothing would change, though, not in the long run. For a few days following, they would make minor efforts before slipping back into the rut of ease that had defined much of their relationship. Then it would start all over, with Antoine being back at square one regretting damn near every decision in his whole damn life that had led to him and Channy hooking up and bringing a baby into the world. He would start thinking about leaving again, which would force Channy to maybe get a job. Helix wouldn't have a father, not a real one anyway, but at least Antoine wouldn't have to listen to all the crying.

The few times Antoine had been left alone with Helix had been rough. The kid was forceful, even though he was only a little baby. Sixteen pounds of determination, that kid. And he always found Antoine lacking—didn't like the way he was being held, or the bottle he was being fed, or the food at the end of the spoon, which he always tried to snatch away or slap at, making a mess of everything. And the crying. Good Lord, the crying. Helix would go on and on and on, and Antoine just wanted him to shut up, even if only for a minute or two. He knew enough to walk away before his temper got the better of him, so he would leave Helix playing on the floor and retreat to the bedroom, thoughts swirling through his head that this was his life now. He'd sit at the foot of the bed sobbing, feeling guilty at the thought of running away and abandoning his girl and his child, and not knowing what else to do, knowing only that he could not live like this. Not for much longer.

On the imagined continuum of Antoine's life, having a kid had not even been a blip on the radar. He had never wanted a kid. Never wanted to get married. Never wanted to be in any kind of long-term relationship. His plan was to go to school, get educated, and get a good job. His grandma had raised him, drumming into him the importance of school, telling him he needed to be a better man this his father—his mother, too, for that matter—and he had to be smart and play smart.

Antoine, who had never known his father and barely knew his mother, had heard enough stories about the both of them to know that being better than either of them could not have been too difficult. Mom was a party girl, dumb as a brick, according to grandma, and into drugs, doing anything to get a fix. Dad had been some random guy mom had hooked up with, and nine months later along came Antoine, dumped with his grandmother.

He supposed that even as a mechanic, he had still done better than either of his parents. He had fallen in love with the sciences as a kid, though, and knew that was something he wanted to pursue. He could be a scientist, or maybe a teacher. Something.

On that continuum was school, first and foremost. Get a degree, get a job.

He'd fucked that up. Then he had made it worse.

The damnedest thing, though, was that he honestly did love Channy and Helix. Their presence in his life was disruptive and intrusive, but more often than not, welcoming. He cared about them, daydreamed about them as he slipped into mindless automation at work, and wanted the best for them both. Sometimes, he just thought that what was best for them was for him to no longer be a part of their lives. Let them find their own ways, enjoy their own freedoms. He was dead weight, and all he would do was drag them down if he stayed. How Channy couldn't see this was beyond him, but there it was. She stuck by him, told him how happy he made her, how perfect their son was because he had helped make Helix.

Trudging through ichor-churned earth, Antoine thought it was about time he told them both how he felt. How he really felt. In the darkness, he swore that he would fight harder to be the man Channy thought he was. Do better, be better. That's what grandma always said. He had been weak, and it was time to change all that.

All he had to do was make it home.

His boot landed in a slick streak of mud and he nearly landed flat on his ass. For what felt like hours, but had probably only been the past five minutes, he had been traveling through another passageway, this one much larger than the previous tunnel between the two domes. He could stand up, but barely. In some places, the ceiling came down unevenly and he had to crouch slightly, but for the most part, he was able to walk comfortably.

The floor, though, was wet and slippery. He couldn't tell what covered the rock floor, only that it was darker than the surrounding walls, and the ground felt spongy beneath his feet. More moss, he suspected. At one point, his boot sank into mud, and a few steps later he splashed through a viscous substance, his foot plunging deep into the liquid.

Best as he could figure, the two previous chambers had been a birthing ground, or maybe a storage room. He shuddered at the implications. The bodies that had hung from the walls and ceiling had looked dead, or near dead, and some—from what limited observations he had been able to make—had been missing parts. His own ear was gone. That got him to thinking that maybe the people were kept there for safekeeping. Unfortunately, he had no idea where this latest passage would lead, and there was only one way to find out.

Several yards down the line, the corridor branched off into three narrow chambers. He could keep going straight, or gamble between the paths to his left and right. Despite the silence, he felt a pressing weight of eyes upon him. He was being watched, although he could not see the creatures. He wished he had a flashlight or a matchbook, something.

After a few moments of indecision, his heart beating loudly enough he worried about the potential for a cave-in, he decided to continue down the middle. If the path petered out or turned into a dead end, he could always turn around and try one of the other tunnels.

As he walked, unseen eyes following his every step, he thought about the tunnels and chambers buried in the earth.

He had no idea how far down below he was, but wandering through this network, sensing the ground gently sloping upward, he couldn't help but think of it being a honeycomb world. Antoine enjoyed reading, and one of his favorite series featured a private detective named Parker. In those books, the author wrote of a honeycomb world, where the supernatural intersected with the everyday. That was what these tunnels reminded him of. The construction and layout of this massive colony, he thought, if one could do a crosscut examination, would look a lot like a beehive, the opening to which had been in the car dealer's showroom floor.

Once he found that opening, that salesman would pay. After being attacked, dropped into some hole in the ground and waking up to a bunch of fucked-up monster bugs, seeing the shit he's seen.... That fat fuck had tried to kill him, had tried to make his baby boy fatherless. Oh yeah, he was going to pay for sure.

TEN

EVEN AS A BOY, Antoine had not been afraid of the dark. The dark was a mysterious presence all of its own, a world full of potential for discovery. The shapes in his bedroom were different in the absence of light, and the night brought on its own life of opposites. In the day, the world was loud and crowded and fast, the lines and curves of life sharply defined beneath the sun. In the night, everything was quiet and slower. The noises in those nighttime hours were ones he never heard in the day—certain birdcalls, like the hooting of owls, or the chirps of crickets. The world possessed an etherealness, the abandoned buildings that made up so much of his everyday lost in pitch, suddenly indistinct and lurking just out of view. He knew they were there, of course, but the night made them a curiosity that was otherwise lacking during the waking hours. Like those deserted buildings in twilight, the darkness was something to be explored, not feared.

Navigating through a tunnel that seemed to be growing tighter and thinner, Antoine found himself afraid. Afraid of what he could feel watching him, afraid of all the things he could not see but knew were there. The hair all over his body stood on end, as if charged by the electric unknown. He wanted to shake his arms and legs, to dance that peculiar icky shuffle, to shake off the web of fright that had snared him and made his spine shiver.

For the first time that he could recall, Antoine was truly fearful of the dark and the things that hid in the shadows and called it home. He had become a quick study in the horrors of the unknown and the ephemeral dangers tucked away in the oppressive confines of the black.

As eyes followed his every footstep, and the tunnel made him crouch deeper and deeper until he was, again, on his hands and knees and crawling through the slimy muck, he had the peculiar sensation that this was how it would feel to be buried alive. The weight of the earth above him was suffocating as the corridor pressed in on all sides.

The noises began again, closer and louder. He could feel them at his heels, following closer now, perhaps emboldened by his confinement. He had no room to kick or swing his bony club. He couldn't flail and shake them loose from his slick, grimy body.

"Oh, God," he whimpered.

A pinprick of pain bloomed in his calf, followed by a warm wetness. Something chittered in appreciation, stabbing at him again. He shoved himself forward, moving as fast as he could. The sound of their pointed limbs pinging on slick rock shattered a piece of his mind. Part of his sanity calved away from his soul and he wanted so badly to scream. A new noise joined the chittering and plinking of chitinous hooks on hard earth, something wet and mewling. After a moment, he realized it was his own whimpering, and his eyes stung with fresh tears.

He wasn't sure if he should laugh or cry, or which would be the easiest path toward the mental breakdown the corners of his mind promised. He now knew why those flimsy remains of nearly dead bodies had laughed so loudly, so madly. Why they had laughed at him. He, too, wanted to laugh. Wanted to let the madness flood through him and embrace it fully. He wanted to laugh nearly as much as he wanted to scream.

Fresh pain jolted through his legs as the creatures found fresh meat in his calves and ankles, biting at his flesh and trying to drag him backward. How easy it would be to surrender, to let them have him again, one last time.

No! he screamed silently, some force in his mind rallying to help push him forward. *Goddammit, no!*

You are going to make it, he told himself. *You are going home. You are going to see your family.*

He kicked back, as best he could, and connected with something solid. The strike was weak, but the creature made a surprised yelp. When he tried to kick a second time, there was only air. He still felt the weight of the bug's presence as he moved forward, its clicking noises following him.

I'm coming home, baby.

He was going to give Helix the longest, tightest hug that boy had ever felt as soon as he saw him. He didn't care if the child was sleeping; he'd risk waking him just to hold him close, and savor the cries of protest as if they were as sweet as the sound of falling rain.

Christ, I've been so fucking stupid, he thought. He vowed, in that tunnel, covered in blood and ichor, to become the embodiment of grandma's words—do better, be better. He was going to be so much better.

Going to hell had been all it had taken for him to realize how stupid and selfish he had been, to see how much he had taken Channy and Helix for granted. He had thought about leaving them both, telling himself it was for their own good, but really it had been his own ugly selfishness rearing its head. He knew that now. He hadn't been ready to be the man they both needed, but, he thought, he certainly would be after this. They both deserved better, but the answer was not to desert them. No, the answer was to be better. To be the man they needed.

Antoine dragged himself forward on his forearms, digging his elbow and toes into the rock and slowly inching his way forward. A single mantra repeated in his mind over and over: *Do better. Be Better. Do Better. Be better. Do better. Be better.*

ELEVEN

DIRT SHIFTED AND FELL down the collar of his coat when it snagged against the earth grazing his back. The passage tightened, the back of his head scraping against the ceiling. He wondered how in the hell the bugs traversed this path, and how, if this was the tunnel he had been transported through earlier, they had gotten him through.

His chest ached as the earth tightened its grip around him and a creeping dread of being buried alive threatened to consume him. The fear passed after a moment as the tunnel opened wider again, and as he passed into a larger chamber, it was as if he'd been birthed into the new opening. Freedom, however, was short lived.

As the earth grew less constrictive, the space filled with bugs. Pale creatures flooded forth, swarming across his body. Splintered limbs gouged a network of trails across his back and limbs, opening fresh wounds. He rolled, attempting to trap what he could beneath him and crush them with his weight. Quick moving shapes darted over his torso and he tried to block quickly stabbing arms from piercing his face.

One of the larger creatures smacked heavily against his chest, its ugly, trapezoidal head nearly touching his own. The petals of its face unfurled to reveal smooth, pink muscles, at the center of which was a pitch black hole festering with barbed teeth. Warm breath struck his face, stinking of putrid, vegetal rot and thick overtones of copper. He pressed his palm into the bug's pointed chin, trying to push it away with one hand while trying to ward off the blows of both of the creature's arms with his other hand.

His efforts were futile.

He smacked away one forelimb, but the bug was surprisingly sophisticated. Antoine was too slow, too tired. He could only watch as a pasty, acicular arm jabbed at his face. His back arched as he screamed, the spiked forelimb spearing his eye. Warm jelly oozed down his face as the orb exploded under the impact. The creature shifted its weight, the needles of its extremities stabbing into his chest and hip, the pain of this lost beneath the stronger currents of misery.

More of the bugs came, washing over his legs and arms. Dimly he was aware of them stabbing at his skull, his remaining eye rolling upward in time to see more wretched faces unraveling to reveal their violently vaginal constructs of a mouth. Their teeth vibrated in the eagerness of hunger.

Blood and salt co-mingled on his lips.

He closed his eye, not wanting his last sight to be a jangling maw reaching toward him. He could feel the weight and warmth of Helix in his arms, the press of Channy's body against his as they made love, and the heat of her kisses against his neck and ears as her hair tickled his face. He could hear his boy's guileless laughter, see the smile that brightened his entire face…

Flesh thudded against flesh, and the creatures around him howled in anger. The weight that had pressed against him was gone. He blinked slowly, unable to grasp what, exactly, had happened.

The creature that had sat upon him was now pinned to the ground beneath a bigger, more thickly muscled monster. When the smaller one shouted its screeching protest, the larger beast slashed at its face, opening an angry welt that bisected its pointed features. They fought, their daggered limbs stabbing into one another, jaws snapping. The smaller bugs, the children of the horde, watched the fight among the elders escalate. They seemed to be waiting for a clear victor, and had grouped themselves into party lines ready to square off against one another should the need arise. Antoine knew his fate hung in the balance, and that he was doomed regardless. He was a prize for whichever side won.

Unless he moved. Unless he took advantage of the creature's infighting and mustered what little energy he had left to run like hell. The devil would be nipping at his heels, so he would have to be quick, and he would have to fight through an awful lot of pain. The sheer agony ripping through his whole body, literally from head to toe, would slow him, which meant he had to be faster than the aching protests.

In the end, there was simply no other choice. The primal calculations of survival whipped through his head reflexively as he got his knees beneath him and half-crawled, half-sprung forward, rapidly working himself up into a run.

Standing, he caught a brief glance of a ruddy, knobbed end of bone. It was the woman's arm he had been carrying as a club. He grabbed it as he launched himself to his feet. Then he ran like hell.

Howls of protest sang out behind him, growing progressively louder and closer. He had his eye, and heart, set on one thing only—the next man-sized tunnel that joined this chamber to whatever lay beyond.

Clods of dirt rained down from above as the creatures scaled the walls and took to the ceiling, racing above him. Their presence behind him was a weight upon his back, one that grew heavier as they neared.

Antoine swung his bone club behind him, felt it connect with something solid, yet pliable, before it was torn loose from his grip and tossed aside.

The tunnel was mere steps away. A dozen steps, and then half a dozen. Five steps. Three steps.

Two steps.

One more step, and he was inside another passageway barely taller than him. Creatures brushed against the back of his head, and, as he unwillingly slowed—exhaustion getting the better of him—a lancet opened the back of his scalp and parted the skin down to a knob of spine between his shoulder blades. The agony spurred him forward, survival instinct urging him to flee ever faster.

His heart was racing, and every drumbeat of the organ ached. His lungs burned, and a cramp blooming beneath his ribs. Drawing in enough oxygen was impossible. The ruined orbit of his lost eye was a cacophony of torment, an unending staccato of fresh misery. But he ran. He ran.

A barbed hook sank into, and then pulled violently away from, his left ass cheek. A scalpel opened his right calf. He wasn't sure if the ripping sound had been his blue jeans or his skin tearing apart. All he knew was to run, even if his running had been reduced to nothing more than a stumbling lurch. He pressed on, unwilling to stop and die.

They were close. Close enough to strike him. Closer than that, now. He could practically feel their stinking breaths pulsing against his back, the brush against his jacket of the petals unfolding from their grotesque mouths.

Ahead was a door.

He could barely believe his eye. He dimly recalled this passage, though. He had seen it briefly, in a flash and then gone, lost to the darkness. Beyond that cold steel door, he knew, were the stairs leading up to the world. The door pulled him forward, compelled him onward. The door possessed its own gravity and was sucking him in, demanding his legs to carry him to it. He ran harder, energized with a second wind and a dull glimmer of hope. Scant inches were all that separated him from the creatures behind him and the door before him.

He reached out, his fingers grasping for the doorknob. The brass was cool against his fever-hot skin, and he breathed a too-early sigh of relief. He turned it. Or tried to. It would not budge. The door shook in its frame and he screamed in frustration.

The bugs barreled toward him, a wave of pale, sickly-looking bodies. When the creatures at the front of the tide leapt toward him, he ducked. Their thuds were marginally satisfying as they struck the door, the wood knocking against its frame, creaking, and then cracking. He kicked at the closest bug, sent it toppling backward as more rammed against him, pressing him against the door. The weight of the pack pushed him back, flattening him against the door, its joints whining a stressful protest. They pushed more, piling against him, and the stressed whine became a fractured splintering.

Antoine fell through the shattered doorframe, too weak to move. Sharp-edged limbs and prickly patches of spikey hair stabbed, jostled, and poked at him. He was disoriented and weak. The adrenaline rush had left him drained, and the blood loss, shock, exertion, and pain had all coalesced into an unstoppable exhaustion. He needed to move. Had to move. If he didn't, he was dead. But he couldn't move, couldn't find the final bit of energy to stave off the inevitable.

Yet the creatures' behavior had changed. There was a palpable sense of hesitancy. The large, thickly muscled bug he had seen earlier stepped forward, its head cocked at a strange angle. The petals of its face twitched and wriggled, and it made an odd chuffing sound. The thing was sniffing the air, its movements slow and cautious as it moved deeper into the chamber.

Antoine realized the bugs had never been this far. The door had been a natural stopping point for their nest, and now they were in unknown territory.

The lead creature approached the stone steps, tentatively stepping upon one. Its kept looking around, constantly surveying its surroundings as if its head were attached to a broken swivel.

Antoine supposed they wanted to be sure there were no other predators around before they consumed their prey, that they would be safe to feast on their victim. But they were also curious, and perhaps much smarter than Antoine had realized. The broken doorway led to a new land, and now they were probably wondering what lay beyond these stairs.

The bugs shifted their attention between the bulkier alpha and Antoine, who lay prone on the earthen ground before the rising steps. Perhaps they sensed a threat of some form, but could not discern exactly where it hid.

His foot was being yanked at by a pair of smaller, hairless creatures. Clearly, they were just infants as their white skin was still stained red from the body they had hatched from. Tugging and biting at his boot, the effect may have been almost comical in another setting. He kicked, shooing them away and earning reproachful hisses from the adults lording over him.

Clicking noises rang through the cavern as the muscular beast proceeded, slowly and one step at a time, up the stone staircase.

TWELVE

"I'M SORRY, MRS. BRANDIS," Dangle said, taking a seat behind his desk, "but this is not a winning ticket."

Mia Brandis was white, forty-eight, and although she was wildly overweight and would provide the Ba'is with a good-sized meal and plenty of leftovers to spare, she was also married and had four children. Her public Facebook account indicated a happy home life and close relations with a bevy of friends and family. Although her credit rating was poor and the photos she had posted of her house indicated a cheap, meager existence in a small brick ranch house with a lawn that was more brown and varying shades of yellow than green, she was also gainfully employed and a regular churchgoer. In other words, if she went missing people would notice.

He tried to hand her back the Money Carlo card, but she waved it off.

"It says right there that I won five thousand dollars," she insisted.

"Well, that was your *potential* winnings," he stressed, "*if* your QR code matched the random generator. Unfortunately, it doesn't, so this is not a winning ticket."

"This is bullshit," she said. Her words were not harsh, blunted with a degree of mournful acceptance. Perhaps life had beaten her down too often and she was used to crushing disappointment as she watched her dreams dissolve. "I don't get *anything*?"

"Well," Dangle said, sheepishly, "anyone who comes in with a losing ticket still wins a two-dollar bill. It's sort of a courtesy prize for dropping by."

"A two-dollar bill? Seriously? That's it?"

Dangle put on his best "oops, you caught me" face. He slid the chair closer to the desk, the casters protesting and the seat squeaking under his shifting weight, and leaned in conspiratorially. "I'm really not supposed to do this, but...." He took a deep breath as he looked past her, eyeing the floor beyond before hunching in closer still. "If you want to look around at the cars, say you see something you like, we could extend you a line of credit equal to what's indicated on your ticket here, good for a down payment on a new vehicle."

"I don't know…"

"Why don't you have a look around? See if anything catches your eye. I noticed your Corolla out there. It looks to be in pretty good condition. I might be able to get you a good deal on a trade-in."

"I'd have to speak with my husband first," she said, cautiously.

"Of course, of course," he said. Mentally, Dangle was already writing her off as a complete loss, as he did with most customers like her, the ones he called one-legged shoppers because they had to lean on their spouse, the old ball-and-chain, for decisions. "Whatever you need to do. If you have any questions, just let me know."

She stood, then paused. Dangle thought he could practically see an extra line of defeat etched into the bags beneath her eyes.

"Do I still get the two dollars?"

Dangle smiled, but it lacked warmth. "Absolutely," he said, unlocking a side drawer on his desk and pulling free a crisp two-dollar bill.

She plucked it from his fingers, folded it in half, and tucked it into her purse. She nodded, mostly to herself, then turned out of Dangle's cubicle. He lost sight of her and expected to never see her again.

A moment later, his phone rang.

"We have a problem," Jensen said. His voice was strained with worry. "You need to come see this."

"What is it?"

"Just get down here."

Dangle took a quick look around the showroom as he left his cubicle and strode down the corridor to the security office. The dealership was by no means packed, but there were a number of browsers milling about the floor, engaged with the other salesmen. Some were killing time while they waited for their car to get serviced with repairs or oil changes. He did not see Mrs. Brandis among them.

He could feel his blood pressure skyrocketing. Jensen never called with an emergency—never. The last time he had heard his brother so shook up was when Jensen had told Jon of their father's passing. Normally, the man was calm, virtually unshakable. For him to sound so nervous made Dangle very, very nervous.

The security door was locked, but Jensen quickly opened up at the sound of the knob rattling. He nearly pulled Dangle inside and off his feet, shoving the door shut behind them and relocking it. Dangle's mouth fell open as he saw why his brother had sounded so strange on the phone.

Splashed across one monitor was the live green-tinged feed of the tunnel beneath them. The Ba'is were there, along with—no. That should not be. *Could not* be. He moved closer to the monitor to study the man's features, which were caked in enough gore to make him nearly unrecognizable. He did recognize the man's clothes, though, and as he peered at what was left of the man's face he was able to determine that it was, in fact, Antoine DeWitt, the man he had dropped into the tunnel three days ago.

"Oh my god," he said, breathlessly.

Standing shoulder to shoulder, the brothers watched as the largest of the Ba'is broke away from the pack, its head studying the surroundings and sniffing at the air. It stepped forward, in that bizarre, halting way of theirs, as if it were some kind of sped-up, stop-motion special effect. It was moving to the stairs, studying them. A pointed limb clicked against the bottom step, darted away, and then returned. It tested its weight, and then shuffled a second leg onto the step, pausing and judging. After a moment, it climbed.

"This is bad," Jensen said.

The Ba'is had never stepped foot into the annex, nor the stairs that connected it from the tunnel to the empty storage room across the hall. Although they had occasionally found their way to the surface by alternate routes, the Ba'is had been largely content with remaining underground and relying on the generations of men in the Dangle family to provide them with food.

In his youth, Dangle had likened them to caged pets. They existed in their own natural conservatory, a terrarium of their own making, and only rarely left it. His father had cuffed him alongside the head and told him not to be stupid.

"They're animals, Jon. Dangerous and wild. We keep them down there, and we feed them, and we pray they never test the boundaries of that arrangement. If they got loose, an awful lot of trouble would follow. But they are not pets. Do not ever think of them as such."

An uneasy alliance existed between the men of his family and the beasts beneath them. As long as the Ba'is were fed, they kept to themselves. If they were denied their feed, they would have to go looking for sustenance, and no doubt many more people would die as a result.

If anything, Dangle saw his actions, and those of his father and those before him, as a sort of community service. They kept the snakes in their cage and gave them no reason to leave it or explore beyond their confines. It was to protect themselves, to protect the Ba'is, and to protect the lives of everyone the Ba'is might otherwise come into contact with.

"Why don't we just kill them?" Jon had once asked.

His father had taken a long moment to collect his thoughts, and Jon nearly spoke again, thinking maybe he hadn't heard. Eventually, his father spoke. "Because they're God's children, Jon. Like you and me. And we don't kill if we don't have to. We would gain nothing by killing them, and we would risk everything by attacking them. Do you understand?"

Dangle did. Going into those tunnels could kill them, and their deaths would break the détente with the Ba'is. Then the creatures would go aboveground. It was impossible to say how large their hive was, how many tunnels were beneath them, and it may never have been possible to root them all out. The family could not guarantee the creature's extinction, so instead they lived with an uncomfortable knowledge that oftentimes required necessary, uncomfortable sacrifices. But they never killed a soul. Every single person they provided the Ba'is with went into the hole alive, and whatever happened to them after that was between the creatures and God himself.

God, it seemed, or at the very least, Antoine DeWitt, had somehow led the Ba'is right to their door, and Dangle was faced with a choice he had worked all his life to avoid. In the end, there was no choice at all, not really. The balance had been upset, and he would have to restore it, or die trying.

On screen, the largest of the Ba'is slammed its weight into the trapdoor above. After repeated attempts, it must have determined the door would not open without assistance. Its head turned, mouth open. Dangle could see its throat ripple, although he could not hear the call it sounded. Seconds later, four more creatures crowded the steps. None were as tall or wide as the initial beast, but that did not matter. When they reared up on their hind limbs, they reached the door easily enough.

After finding the right key on his keyring, he unlocked one of the wall-mounted cabinets. Inside was an array of guns and ammunition clips. He pulled down a .357 Sig Sauer P226 Nitron, inserted the magazine, and pocketed several more.

Maybe they'll give up, he hoped. If the door proved too difficult, or better still, too painful to bash open, the Ba'is would file back down the stairs and refocus their attention on Antoine DeWitt where it belonged. Dangle hoped for the best, but knew better than to rely on it with nothing more than blind faith.

"We need to evacuate. Get everybody out of here."

Jensen nodded. He triggered the building's internal alarm system, which was noisy and set off flashing lights all through the showroom, but which was not connected to a central dispatch service. No police or fire services would be notified, but the blaring alarm was annoying enough to clear people out of the building. Jensen would make sure they left the premises entirely. Hopefully none of them would call 911 in a fit of presumptive helpfulness.

"Tell them authorities have already been notified," Dangle said.

"I'm on it," Jensen said, halfway out of the room.

The door softly clicked shut. Dangle's attention was consumed entirely by the surveillance monitor and the unrelenting assault of Ba'is against the trapdoor. A body tensed, leapt up from the step, its monstrous head crashing into the door above, and then—

It was gone.

The Ba'is stood still for a moment, then joined their leader into the space above.

He could not hear them assaulting the door of the storage room across the hall over the raging fury of the building's alarm, but he was positive they were seeking a way out of that room now, too. The Ba'is were inside, aboveground, and soon they would discover the world.

THIRTEEN

THE CAVITY OF ANTOINE'S missing eye burned a raging inferno of agony. A tightness gripped his ankle as one leg lifted, the skin dimpling beneath his blue jeans, caught in the creature's pincers, and then hard tugging pulled at his foot. It felt like the monster was trying to tear his foot off.

But, no. Not his foot. His shoe. The heel of it came away, then got stuck at an awkward angle against his own heel, his toes crimpling against the underside of the tongue, tight laces locking it in place. More yanking, more pulling. He didn't care. He hurt too much to care.

A crack of splintering wood sounded out loudly in the darkness. A hearty thud of meat against solid planking, nails clicking on stone. The noises repeated, the cracking growing louder. Their noises—their screeches and howls, like pigs getting gut shot—stabbed at the inside of his skull, his ears aching.

Then they went suddenly, maddeningly, quiet.

He strained his neck to follow their progress. The large one jumped through the hole it had made in the trapdoor situated at the top of the staircase, and was followed by a second and third. More banging noises followed, and then—

What sounded like the obnoxious bleating of a very loud alarm system. Followed by—

A gunshot! Close enough that it rang out over the alarm. Then—screams.

Antoine could not make out the words, but he could hear the panicked shouts, muted beneath the wailing warble of the dealership's siren.

One of the creatures glared down at him, then swiveled its head away and charged toward the stairs. The younglings followed, racing up the stone risers and, when room on the stairs ran out, along the walls on either side. Their hairs scraped against him as their pale forms whispered past.

Antoine was alone, half-blind, the polluted sounds of shock and pain and high-pitched electronic shrieking filtering down to him from a distant place somewhere far above.

He reached forward, his muscles resistant but he forced them to comply, and kicked with a leg. This motion helped to resituate his shoe, even as it pushed him along the ground. He repeated it with the opposite set of limbs, inching his way ahead to the steps. He was so exhausted, bone-deep exhausted, that he did not want to stand. Again, he forced his muscles to do the work, made his legs bend and carry him up. He leaned, half-resting against the wall beside him for support, but he climbed. Slowly, yes, but surely nonetheless, he climbed.

He rose into an empty room, facing an open door. Beyond was a crisp, bright splash of red against a white wall. The cacophony hurt his ears, made him disoriented. He lurched forward, practically collapsing against the doorframe.

He could see clearly down the length of the corridor, straight into the showroom. What he saw was hell on Earth.

FOURTEEN

SLOWLY, DANGLE OPENED THE security room door, enough to peek through the crack. The hallway was empty, and he had a clear line of sight to the storage room. The door jostled in its frame, the rattling growing more furious by the second.

He stepped into the hall, the Sig Sauer pointing ahead of him, tucked in close to his body. He quickly looked both ways down the hall, saw that it was clear, and moved to the storage room.

The door burst outward, shattering with explosive force. Shards of wood peppered his face. One of the Ba'is pounced through the hole, knocking Dangle off his feet. He rolled, bringing the gun up and fired into the thick thorax of the beast. The bullet went high, striking the large monstrosity near its shoulder.

A flash of movement caught his eye as Jensen rushed toward him and the creatures. More of them were pouring out the entryway, too much of a blur to count.

Jensen let out a scream as he punched at the creature, driving it away from Dangle.

"Get out of the way," Dangle yelled.

The Ba'is reared on its hind legs, its forelimbs rising in a manner similar to a praying mantis preparing to fight. Its barbed, pointed limbs fell, impaling Jensen through the chest. Again, it reared back and twisted at the middle, hauling Jensen off his feet and flinging him aside. A bold red streak painted the white wall and Jensen fell, unmoving. Blood dripped from the insectile thing's appendages as it briefly studied its surroundings. When it caught sight of Dangle, still sitting on the floor, gun raised, the flaps concealing the anatomy of its face rippled open and it let out a treacherous, high-pitched cry.

Dangle's bladder spasmed, a warm current running down the inside of his thighs. The wet crotch of his underwear clung to his balls, his pants sodden.

The beast let out another cry, and for a brief moment Dangle thought he saw something reflected in its prism of eyes. Contempt, perhaps, or maybe simple, mocking laughter. Even with a bullet wound in its trunk, the creature still found Dangle inferior. The hairs on its legs bristled against his bare arms as it moved past him, leaving him furiously itchy.

Screams drew his attention to the showroom. People were still inside, and they were confronted with what had to have been more than a dozen of the strange beings.

A blonde woman, cell phone in hand, backed up along the front of a bright, waxy blue Corvette. When her heel struck the car's tire, she nearly toppled onto the hood but caught herself. Her rump rested on the rounded contours of the hood, four of the Ba'is encircling her and jabbing at her with long, dangerous limbs. She kicked at them, her floral-patterned skirt billowing out and taking an extra second to settle back into place as she got both feet back on the ground. Another prod was followed by another kick. They were toying with her. The Ba'is looked back and forth between themselves and the woman, and as Dangle drew closer he could hear their noisy clicking. One of the Ba'is shuffled in closer and she swung her handbag at its face, but came up too short to make contact. The creature reared back, but Dangle saw the woman's error as she turned toward this fresh opening between them. She was completely oblivious to how they were flanking her, unaware that the beast she had lashed out at was little more than a distraction. From above, one of the Ba'is bounded down atop her, tackling her onto the hood of the Corvette. A moment later, her face was lost inside the rippling digits of the monster's maw. Another Ba'is rushed in, grabbing at her kicking legs. She had lost one shoe already and her bare foot disappeared into the creature's mouth. Yet another Ba'is approached, folding its serrated arm around her other leg. As she kicked, the barbs split open the length of her calf, blood sheeting down her leg and over the beast's pale skin.

As three Ba'is dismembered the blonde, the fourth appeared to be studying its siblings gorging themselves, its head cocked at an awkward angle. Hunched beside the front wheel well of a Tahoe, Dangle lined up the gunsights and fired. The monster's head vanished in a pulpy mess as ichor spattered against the vehicle, its brethren seemingly undisturbed as they went about their feeding. What was left of the woman had stilled, her one remaining arm splayed loosely across the hood as if she had reached out in one last attempt at escape, or out of surrender.

Despite the blaring siren, Dangle could still hear the pained shouts of those dying around him. The showroom had become a freakish tableau straight out of a Salvador Dali painting. Dead bodies limply folded atop cars, or were left gutted on the floor. The largest of the Ba'is had a man pinned to the wall, its forelimbs shot through the man's shoulders and embedded into the plaster behind him. Its head was lost inside the man's belly, a rope of intestines dangling from his gut to spool upon the carpet. Face slack, his mouth hung open in a rictus of a lapsed cry. He was clearly dead, and for that Dangle was grateful.

Dangle's stomach bobbed and weaved, upending his morning snack. Acidic coffee burned its way up his throat, and he turned, barely in time to avoid upchucking all over his lap. Globs of bile and chunks of masticated, unidentifiable food slumped in the liquid. He felt sweaty and ill, and knew all too well how stupid he had been.

He swiped the drool away from his lips, and then forced himself to look back at the horrific landscape surrounding him. The three Ba'is were still carving into the woman on the Chevrolet. They were the closest, and perhaps, as a result, the easiest targets. He took careful aim, dispensing them one by one. He took care of the creatures positioned around what were left of her legs first, and when they fell away, he saw they had made impressive work. The meat of her thighs had been torn away, right down to the bone. He then targeted the central mass of the bulky beast gorging on the woman's face. When the Ba'is slumped, its body flattening against hers, he was grateful he couldn't see what was left of her head, grateful that perhaps the worst of it was buried beneath the creature's carcass.

How the hell do I stop this? he wondered. His hands shook, and even under the noxious stench of violent death he was struck by his own rotten odor of vomit, piss, and sweat. The back of his shirt was caked to his shoulders, he was sweating so profusely.

Four, he thought, *that's four dead.*

What he saw on display all around him left little room for encouragement. At least a dozen more of the creatures were arrayed around the showroom carnage, and it appeared he was the last person alive. The customers had been slaughtered, the receptionist torn apart, and the remains of what he guessed were his two salesmen were scattered messily across freshly waxed cars and desktops.

And Jensen. Oh, Jesus, Jensen.

He couldn't afford to shut his eyes and mourn his brother. He was the last one alive, and he had to take care of this. Things had gotten out of hand so quickly, and he had no idea how many more Ba'is lurked below ground, how many could be making their way to the surface. He could not allow any more of them to reach the surface.

He swallowed, his mouth desert dry.

He looked toward the hallway, readying himself to run back to the security room and—

Pain exploded in his face as his nose smashed inward and deflated beneath a rough, thick fist. He had turned right into the punch.

For a brief moment, he was glad for the agony, glad to see it was a human standing over him. He was not alone. Antoine DeWitt stood over him. The man punched him a second time, hard enough to loosen several of his front teeth so that, on the third punch, they fell away entirely. Although his mouth was filled with blood, Jon Dangle couldn't help but smile.

FIFTEEN

THE SICK MOTHERFUCKER WAS grinning at him like a goddamn fool, laughing at him even now.

"Fuck you," Antoine screamed, sending another quick jab into the man's ruined face. The fucker's lips were already swelling. He delivered another punch, going for the salesman's eyes, pounding down on him over and over and over. His fists did the job, but his punches weren't what they should have been. He was too tired to tenderize this flabby fuck the way he'd earned.

The salesman slumped back against the Tahoe, his eyes glassy. He'd lost his grip on the gun, and Antoine couldn't think of any reason for this son of a bitch to not be relieved of his weapon. The grip had fallen into a filthy puddle of puke. Antoine had to wipe it off as best he could on the man's pants, down low by his ankle since much of the upper half of his trousers were soaked with piss. In the long run, Antoine figured it didn't much matter. He was caked, head to toe, in so much filth that handling a puke-covered gun was the least of his troubles.

"You son of a bitch," Antoine said, taking in the full scope of the depravity around him. "You son of a bitch! You did this all this!"

At first, the man tried to shake his head, to deny it, but he stopped abruptly. He was staring at a far-off point in the distance behind Antoine, and then he nodded. His nod turned into tears.

Antoine reached down and grabbed him by the front of his shirt, too weak to haul him to his feet. Instead, the salesman's ass rose off the ground and he toppled forward. Antoine dragged him back down the hallway.

"There's a secure room," the man painfully muttered, waving toward the room. He didn't even try to fight Antoine's pull.

Antoine had half a mind to toss the sleazy fucker into the empty room with the hole in the ground and hope that more of these creatures were on their way, hungry enough to eat up this motherfucker. Maybe shoot him in the kneecaps first, so he couldn't climb back up the stairs.

He pushed through the security door, hauling the bastard in behind him, and then slammed and locked the door. The salesman lay on the ground, useless.

On the monitors, the creatures ate.

"I'm sorry," the man eventually said.

Antoine looked down at him. "This is all your fault, you know that?"

"I do. I know."

"You tried to kill me. Tried to make my son fatherless. Cost me my eye. You know how much I bled because of you? Do you even understand the kind of torment you put me through? And for what?"

The car salesman coughed out a dry chuckle, devoid of humor. "For what? The 'what' was to prevent this"—he waved at the monitors—"all of this, from happening. We feed them, and they stay belowground. We sacrifice so that others never have to."

"What the fuck do you think you've ever sacrificed?" Antoine shouted.

The gun was astoundingly heavy in Antoine's hand. He had to drag it into the air, the act of aiming the barrel and centering it on the man's chest a complex and exhausting endeavor. He'd never killed anyone before. Had never even fired a gun before. Still, he knew the basics. Point and shoot. And that you never pointed a gun at a man unless you intended to use it.

A ring of fire roared through his head, centered in the hole where his eye had once been. Sweat stung his remaining eye, his vision clouded by a standing pool of salty tears. His pain was not just bone-deep, but soul deep. His heart ached in all the ways he thought impossible.

With his finger on the trigger, he thought of Helix and Channy. He missed them, and that made the sting of his tears more awful. On the floor before him was the man who had ripped him away from his family, his two loves. A man who would have left an aching hole in their lives, bigger and worse than all the aches Antoine felt.

"How do I stop them?" Antoine asked, nodding toward the carnage unfolding on the television.

"You can't."

Antoine spent a moment absorbing that information, then shrugged. "Guess I don't need you, then."

He fired once into the center of the large man's chest. The white shirt turned crimson, nearly black, as the stain quickly spread; a moment later, he was dead.

Antoine stared down at the corpse. He had expected to feel some sense of satisfaction, perhaps a measure of closure. Instead, he felt nothing other than a minor tremble in his hand. Dangle's murder had been a hollow affair that left Antoine empty. He was too exhausted, too beaten down, to feel any guilt over the taking of a life.

He just wanted to go home. Even the hospital could wait, if only for a little while longer. He needed to feel Helix in his arms, needed to hold Channy.

Looking toward the monitors, though, he knew his family would have to wait. He had one more job to do, and he needed to figure out how to do it.

All of the cabinets lining the walls were locked, and he went digging around in the dead man's pockets to find the key. Unlocking a wall-mounted cabinet, he whistled at the arsenal before him. In terms of artillery, there were mostly pistols and some rifles, and a small box with hand grenades neatly lined up in a black foam shell case. He couldn't tell what was what, but he recognized an AR-15, which he had seen plenty of on the news. It looked much bigger in real life, even more intimidating than on television. There was always some kind of story about a crazy white guy shooting up a nightclub, or a school, or women's clinic with that gun.

He figured out how to eject the magazine in the pistol, pointing the gun away from himself. The last thing he needed was to accidentally shoot himself in the balls with it. He'd found other magazines in the salesman's pockets, so he'd taken those as well. He also took the man's wallet, which had a couple hundred dollars in it and a swipe card with a logo Antoine recognized as being for the dealership's fuel management company. He inserted a fresh magazine, and then tucked the gun into the back of his waistband. He slung the strap for the AR-15 over his shoulder and pocketed all the bullets he could carry.

He rummaged in the other desk drawers and cabinets for anything that might be of use. He started on the left-hand side of the desk, quickly working through the three pullouts and finding nothing of use. He moved onto the center drawer and rifled through the pens and sticky notes. He had a sliver of a plan forming, but he needed—

There! A BIC lighter, one of the disposable kinds. The transparent red case showed there was still plenty of lighter fluid inside.

Maybe this will work.

He pocketed the lighter, then checked the camera feed. The hallway still looked clear, with the creatures all gathered in the showroom. If he was going to leave, now was the time to do it.

Upon opening the door, he turned down the hall, heading in the opposite direction from the showroom and toward the bright red EXIT sign at the rear of the building. A warning stated that the door was for emergency use only, and that opening it would trigger an alarm. He decided he was fine with that and shoved his way through. True enough, an alarm did sound, mingling with the other, louder siren in a disparate and unharmonious racket.

Sunlight blinded him briefly as he stumbled into a sales lot filled with the on-hand stock of Chevrolets of all makes and models, all from within the last year. His eyes cleared and he made his way around the side of the building, remembering the sign he had seen for the dealership's service bay when he had walked in a whole other lifetime ago.

Antoine pulled open the door to the service bay, tucking the stock of the AR-15 into his shoulder as he stepped through. The seating area was empty, as was the space behind the counter where the clerks checked customers in and out. He walked to the end, to a swinging half-door, and shoved his way through into the employees' area, then into to the mechanics' bay. No signs of life in there, either.

Clearly the staff and customers had gotten the gist of what was happening and took off, compelled either by the siren or the creatures to get their asses outta there. The fact that nobody stayed behind to woolgather and gossip while they watched the dealership transform into a slaughterhouse told him all he needed to know. If anyone had gone into the showroom to help or to collect a spouse or whatever, they were dead now. He was alone in here. Perfect.

The service bay was sleek and shiny, clean looking. Each of the six bays was occupied with a vehicle up on a hydraulic lift. He spent a few minutes looking around, and eventually found what he needed.

A mechanic himself, Antoine knew motor oil required very high temperatures, in excess of four hundred degrees, to release and ignite the liquid's vapors. Gasoline, on the other hand, was extraordinarily flammable, even in cold temperatures. Safety meant they could not keep gas in the service bay, but he did find several empty Briggs & Stratton fuel containers and a handful of cloth towels. He carried three cans, one stuffed under his arm with the collection of towels, and headed back outside to a massive gas tank at the rear of the parking lot, well away from the building.

Clear blue skies, bright yellow sun, and mostly quiet other than some bird calls and the dull roar of the building's alarms. He set the gas cans down, then searched his coat pockets for the salesman's wallet and withdrew the gas card. The pump had an electronic swipe reader, and accepted the card immediately. The digital display changed from a yellow and black welcome screen to a single word: PASSWORD.

"Shit," he hissed.

There were four dashes on screen, which meant it was a four-digit code. He tried 1-2-3-4.

INCORRECT
PASSWORD

The dashes returned a heartbeat later.

He looked at the man's driver's license and entered the man's birth year. 1-9-7-3.

INCORRECT
PASSWORD

Anxiety twisted through his gut. The house number was four digits. 4-9-0-1.

INCORRECT
PASSWORD

"God damn it!"

The screen returned to the welcome message. Antoine swore again, fighting to recollect his cool, but his nerves were shot. This had to work. It had to!

He swiped the card again. The machine returned to the password prompt. He dug through the interior pockets of the wallet, hoping for a clue. Something, anything, that could tell him what the numbers were. He pulled out one the man's business cards. There were three phone numbers listed: one for the dealership, a mobile number, and the fax machine. There was also a business e-mail, but it contained no numbers, just his name, first and last separated by a period.

He tried the last four digits of the man's cell phone, and swore again when it failed. He wanted to punch the fucking machine, but forced himself to breathe. His nostrils flared as he exhaled. He entered the final numbers of the dealership number.

5-4-3-0.

INSERT NOZZLE INTO
GAS TANK AND SELECT

YOUR FUEL GRADE

"Oh holy shit. Oh, god, thank you, Jesus!"

He set about filling up the gas cans. Rather than screw the dispenser nozzle back on, he wadded up the end of a cloth towel and stuffed one into each hole. Carefully, he walked back to the dealership, up the front steps outside the clear glass-fronted showroom.

The dealership's austerity had been lost beneath ugly smatterings of gore. Nearly a dozen bodies littered the ground, or were draped over vehicles. The bright shininess had been blanketed in red. Innards littered the ground. A few limbs had been tossed aside, but he could not discern whom they had once belonged to.

All of the creatures were still there, best he could tell. If anything, there were more than when he had left. He had not been gone long, but they had been busy. Already, some of the victims were being hauled to the far side of the showroom, but Antoine shuddered to think for what purpose. Others were held to the wall by a collection of the creatures, who were spitting up a thick, brownish paste across their victims' limbs. Immediately, he recognized they were creating a new hive. Those pasted to the wall, or the walls of cubicles, were still alive. Barely, perhaps, but still breathing despite all the physical damage they had suffered.

"Fuck," he whispered.

Nothing had changed, though. He still had to do this.

Quietly, he slipped in through the central entrance and set the gas cans down. He flicked the BIC, watching the creatures as they worked. None had taken an interest in him yet. He touched the flame to one of the rags, then grabbed the can and threw it into the center of the hoard. A small fireball exploded in the air as the vapors leapt up and erupted. Gasoline arced through the air, and then burst out of the container when it thumped into the ground. The fire spread quickly, sending panic through the creatures. Their hairs caught and sparked, driving them into wild hysterics.

Antoine aimed down the rifle sights, picking off as many of the monsters as he could. He had gotten lucky with that throw, but the bugs were fast. Too damn fast. They scrabbled up the wall, onto the drop ceiling. He followed what he could with the rifle, shooting off rapid bursts, missing most of them.

He stopped firing long enough to light up another Molotov, and flung it into the depths of the showroom. The bugs gave off a rotten stink as they burned, his nose crinkling under the gut-curdling stench.

With the third gas can, he decided to remove the rag and started shaking fuel out and onto the floor. A trio of bugs dropped from the ceiling right in front of him, and were caught with a passing wave of gasoline. The fumes and coolness of the liquid clearly aggravated them, and they reared back in unison, their fishhook teeth clacking loudly, close enough that he could hear the chittering of their mouths and their unnatural screams, beneath the sirens.

He threw the empty can at them, and, in a surprisingly fluid movement, pulled the pistol from his waistband. He fired point-blank into their faces, multiple shots to each ugly mug. They fell hard, the stench of gasoline thick in the air. He flicked the BIC again and tossed it into the center of the gas-soaked bug corpses. They erupted into flames immediately, an awful burning stinkbug odor gagging him and driving him back. He tripped over the strip of welcome carpeting at the door as he scrambled backward.

Cool air greeted him, and he continued to kick his way back. Flames flickered in the glass as he stood and raced down the steps. Approaching sirens cut through the blue skies. A caravan of firetrucks and police cruisers raced down the forested road, turning into the dealership's lot and screeching to a halt.

As he turned toward the vehicles, police burst from their cars, rapidly drawing their guns and taking aim at Antoine. He immediately began to raise his hands in surrender, aware that he was still carrying the rifle, that he still had the pistol in his hands.

At least that is what he had tried to do, anyway.

His hand barely raised past his hip when he saw the flash of gunfire. Police were shouting, at him, at one another, their voices lost in a swelter of aggressive yelling. Another flash caught his eye, and another. Pain exploded in his left shoulder, a second blossom of agony in his belly, staggering him back on his feet. His legs suddenly felt rubbery, his knees buckling, unable to keep his body erect. He stumbled, his ankle turning painfully, and his ass hit the ground. Another bullet slammed into his chest, another in his thigh, just as he was falling. He saw blood eject from the meat of his quadriceps, felt the bone explode.

Don't let me die now. Not like this. Not like this.

Half a dozen police rushed forward, their movements a blur. Antoine could barely see straight, his mouth filled with an awful coppery taste. A red bubble popped against his lips. He couldn't just lay there and die, though. He still had one good, working leg, and he dug his heel into the ground, pushing uselessly backward. Concrete scraped his back raw. He was only dimly aware of the heavy press of a solid object in his hand. He couldn't believe it, couldn't believe it at all. He still had the gun, somehow, and a curious part of his mind began to raise the numb, useless arm.

"Oh shit!" somebody shouted.

The sky erupted again with a flurry of gunshots that left Antoine deafened. A quieter noise peeled through the air, beneath the sirens, at the very edge of his hearing. After a too-long moment, he realized it was the sound of his own agonizing screaming. Wet sludge lodged in his throat, choking him, each hacking effort a grueling drain that left his face spattered with a thick, near-black liquid.

Sluggishly, his fingers fell away from the gun. A boot hit his ribs hard, and he heard metal skitter against concrete as the cop kicked the pistol out of his reach. Another officer tugged at his chest, and he dimly realized the rifle was being hauled away from him.

The edges of the world were dissolving into black, and his eyelid was very, very heavy. Still, he managed to find the gaze of a nearby policeman and met his eyes. He hoped for one last bit of human contact before he died, but all he saw was anger and malice. Clear intent lived in that officer's eyes, and on his lips were a hint of a smile. An inhuman shout broke their stare. The officer turned toward the sound, while another cop screamed, "What the fuck!"

Antoine tried to turn his head, interested in what had distracted the police, but the movement was too difficult. Ultimately, his skull slumped to the side, blood pouring from his mouth to puddle against the pavement. Before him was the flickering of fire and the movement of shadows behind the glass entry.

Oh, Channy…Helix…I'm sorry. I am so goddamn sorry. So, so sorry!

A windowpane exploded outward as a large creature coated in fire leapt through. Its screams commanded the attention of the police, who turned to open fire. The creature howled, rushing toward the lawmen, daggered limbs snapping outward.

One cop was lanced through the throat, his head popping off like a plucked grape. His fellow officers were firing at the creature, its hind legs backpedaling, hauling the dead cop with it. It had caught fresh prey and was not letting go. Smoke roiled off its body, ichor sizzling off the heat of its ruined flesh. The beast slowed, raised one arm, and lashed out at another uniform. It cut a large slash down the officer's shirt, revealing the Kevlar vest beneath.

The creature stuttered backward, howling. Its eyes were gone, blasted away by the police officers' guns. Its chest rippled under the assault, and then it fell. Its legs collapsed beneath it, its bloody thorax doubling over as its head slumped, then crashed to the ground.

"What the fuck?" one of the cops was shouting. "What the fuck? What the fuck? What the—"

Antoine lay very still, arms spread out to either side of him. His whole body felt freezing cold, all except for the side of his face open to the loving touch of the sun.

He closed his eye and let exhaustion claim him.

SIXTEEN

LAURA MEYERS HAD A sexy voice, but a face and body made for radio. Dr. Joseph Alder had looked her up on the NPR website once before, and found himself severely disappointed. Still, that voice. He could listen to her talk all day, even if the topics were as ludicrous as the protest she was currently covering.

Outside City Hall, less than a hundred protestors were gathered, complaining about what they thought was an unlawful shooting of yet another black man armed to the teeth. The very same black man, now very much unarmed and unclothed, was lying on the autopsy table before him now.

Dr. Alder, along with Antoine DeWitt's body, was in the smaller of the two autopsy rooms, one that was typically used for homicides because it could be closed off from the rest of the medical examiner's office to limit the number of prying eyes and curious busybodies in the secretary pool. Given the nature of DeWitt's death and the odd circumstances surrounding the crime scene at the car dealership, the less prying eyes the better.

On the radio behind him, Meyers was interviewing one of the protestors, a woman who kept dropping the phrase Black Lives Matter.

Christ, Alder huffed. *Don't these people have anything better to do?*

Most of the protestors, from what he had seen on the local news, weren't even coloreds. They were ignorant college kids with too much time on their hands and an overly large sense of entitlement, as far as he could tell. And besides, didn't *all* lives matter? He sighed deeply. Of course, if Alder were being perfectly honest with himself, he would have to admit that, no, not all lives mattered, either.

DeWitt's flesh was pale, puckered by nearly a dozen bullet wounds peppering his chest, arms, and legs. If anything, Alder thought the cause of death would be easy enough to discern. Still, the procedure would be time consuming and he would have to collect fluids and tissue samples.

The police were claiming DeWitt had opened fire on them with both an assault rifle and a handgun, and that they had acted in self-defense. The officers involved, or rather those that had been involved in the shooting and had lived through the…the attack, he supposed was the best term for what had occurred, were on paid leave pending the results of the investigation. Alder expected to find plenty of drugs and alcohol in DeWitt's system.

Last night, Alder had sat up in his bed watching the eleven o'clock news on his wall-mounted flat-screen television set. A perky blonde had been reporting from outside the scorched remains of an auto dealership, police tape flapping in the breeze behind her. Past the tape were a score of police cars. He paid little attention to the reporter's words, watching, instead, as police and Alder's own team of medical examiners entered the showroom in groups. One group went in, another came out. Sometimes they carried large cardboard boxes, and other times two men would pass the camera carrying black body bags between them. Alder had not been present at the scene yesterday, and he was grateful for it. According to the police, DeWitt had shot and killed all of the employees present at the car dealership, along with a number of customers and several police officers. He knew, too well, that he would soon be seeing the bodily aftermath of such carnage.

One of the technicians had already recorded DeWitt's height, weight, hair, and eye color when the decedent had first arrived the previous evening. Alder prided himself on his thoroughness, though, and thought it best to double-check. He would have hated for there to be a fucking clerical error over something so basic. With DeWitt's spouse already threatening a lawsuit before the man's body was even cold, neither he nor his team could be responsible for giving a legal defense team a single shred of meat to chew on. Especially not over something so clearly open and shut.

He stepped on the metal plate that activated the digital scale to weigh the deceased. He read off the display: 198.6 lbs. Pen at the ready, he turned to the clipboard where the technician had already written 190.8 lbs.

Cheeks flushing red, Alder hissed at the mistake.

Goddammit. Good thing I checked.

And then the display changed.

198.8.

Fuck.

That was all he needed now. A malfunctioning scale. He stepped off the metal plate, then turned off the scale and gave it to the count of ten just to be on the safe side. Then, he stepped back onto the wiggling plate.

199 pounds.

He watched the numbers, fully expecting them to change. After a moment, he jotted down the corrected weight, mentally cursing computers and mankind's dependency on the error-prone pieces of shit.

On the chart before him was a picture showing the general outline of the human body. DeWitt's visible injuries had already been noted, but Alder went through it again. If the idiot technician could not even get the weight right, he doubted the woman could draw a rough approximation of a gunshot wound on a sheet of paper. Surprisingly, though, the technician's work seemed to match the specimen before him, right down to the missing eye, missing ear, and absent digit.

Good for her.

He set the chart aside and began to inspect DeWitt's body. Aside from the dozen or so entry wounds, the man's torso and limbs were littered with cuts, some shallow, some remarkably deep, and—

Now that's odd, he thought. The man's belly was distended, and when he pressed a gloved finger to the area he felt a strange hardness beneath the tissue. He pressed gingerly, and then yanked his hand back. Whatever was beneath DeWitt's flesh moved. The distended lump lowered, then rose up half an inch higher, the skin pulsing. Alder was reminded of a pregnant woman's baby pressing against the stomach, and he recalled the first time he had felt his baby boy kicking inside his ex-wife.

He thought about the news broadcast and the strange, conflicting rumors his staff spoke of in hushed whispers. DeWitt had tripped on some type of new, hardcore drug and went insane, and then went on a crazed shooting spree— that's what the cops said, and the District Attorney had even called Alder personally to strongly suggest the same. Somewhere along the way, though, somebody had mentioned bugs, hadn't they? He had heard somebody whisper about bugs as he was getting his first allotment of mandatory daily caffeine, somebody who'd heard from a friend who'd heard from a cop, or some such nonsense. Rumors and rumormongering—nonsense, the whole lot of it.

"Ba'is," somebody had said. "That's what the Injuns are saying over at the casino." Alder had heard the name before, but couldn't recall where or how he had come by it. The creatures were a local legend, like the Michigan Dogman over in Wexford, or the Loch Ness Monster. Occasionally, a crackpot or tourist would claim they had seen a monster out in the woods or out by the abandoned salt mine. One had even claimed to spot something strange during a midnight golfing session at the Bear, but he had been both trespassing and high as a kite. Bullshit, all of it.

But then something in DeWitt's abdomen shifted again.

Alder took a deep breath, inhaling the heady perfume of disinfectants, the light ammonia-like odor of formalin, and, beneath all of that, a sweet and musty metallic stink. He raised the scalpel and cut the first line of the branching Y-incision, starting at the top of one shoulder and cutting down, around the navel, to the pubic bone. No blood seeped from the incision until the scalpel cut down DeWitt's stomach, and then a thick, black ichor welled into the gap.

"What the hell?" Alder said. Fully aware of the voice-activated recorder cataloging his words, he added, "There is a thick fluid pooling along the line of the incision at Mr. DeWitt's stomach, and—"

Words failed him as long, slender limbs wormed through the thin gap and began to push apart either side of the cut. A serrated limb snapped out of the opening, then another, the thing's forelimbs gripping either side of the corpse's trunk as it pulled itself forward. A pale, gore-mottled cone pressed against the surface of flesh beside DeWitt's hip and rose from his stomach, its lips parted around a mouthful of organ meat clenched between bear-trap-like teeth.

Alder's fingers went limp and the scalpel clinked against the floor several times before it finally settled and went still. Behind the plastic facemask, his mouth hung open and his eyes felt two sizes too large for his skull. He stepped backward, hands already up in the universal gesture for *stop*, in case the insectoid monstrosity spoke the same primitive ASL.

The white creature slid wetly away from the cavity, and in that moment, Alder gasped. A clutch of eggs were deposited within DeWitt's belly, filling the spaces between organs, settled amidst the loops of intestine.

The nightmare before him perched atop DeWitt's split torso like a gargoyle. It was on him in a flash. Its razor-bladed limbs stabbed into Alder's eyes, blinding him instantly.

He screamed as something sharp pulled, and then tore at his flesh, ripping apart the skin on his face, tearing away his cheeks and gnashing at his throat. Long, pointed limbs dug into his skull and chest as the creature mounted and gripped him, finding all the soft spots around Alder's cranium and slurped wetly at all there was to feast on.

Although he could not see any longer, and despite his own agonizing shrieks, Alder could still hear. In those final moments, as he quickly bled out upon death's doorway, he heard a soft, almost gentle, cracking noise. It took his blood-starved brain a moment to process the sound, but after an instant it came to him.

It was the sound of eggs hatching, and the noise of these pale, ugly, underground things, these *rumors*, finding their way into the light.

A NOTE TO READERS

Thank you for choosing to read my work – it is greatly appreciated and I hope you enjoyed the journey.

If you be willing to spare a minute or two, please leave a brief review of this work and let other readers know what you thought. Reviews are incredibly helpful, particularly for an independent author and publisher such as myself, and can help determine the success of a novel. Reviews do not need to be long – twenty words or so should suffice – but their impact can be enormous.

I look forward to your thoughts, and thank you, once again, for taking the time to read this story.

If you would like to know about upcoming releases, I encourage you to subscribe to my newsletter at http://michaelpatrickhicks.com.

And if you enjoyed this book, please consider joining me on Patreon, where readers receive copies of all my stories and novels every month. Patreon members get all of my work first, before anyone else. For more information, visit: http://www.patreon.com/michaelpatrickhicks

ACKNOWLEDGEMENTS

I began writing this story in the summer of 2016, and it went through numerous drafts before it grew into a work I was comfortable with. Even then, though, it felt like something was missing, and I needed a fresh pair of eyes on it.

KC Santo provided those fresh eyes, as well as a fresh outlook on the material that, by the time a previous version of this manuscript made its way to her, I was otherwise lacking. Frankly, I would have been hard-pressed to find a better beta reader, and KC gave me an abundance of feedback, all of which helped shape and transform this book into something far superior than it had originally been. KC – I really cannot thank you enough!

In addition to providing a superb critique, KC is also a greatly valued Patreon supporter, alongside Kate Martyniouk. Their generosity, as well those of my other Patreon patrons help make my work possible with their monthly pledges.

Shay VanZwoll, owner and operator of EV Proofreading, edited this manuscript, provided feedback and encouragement, and cleaned up (or at least helped to hide) plenty of my mistakes. Any errors that remain are all mine!

Thanks, also, to Kealan Patrick Burke for the snazzy cover. In addition to being an awesome artist, Kealan is also a Bram Stoker Award winning horror author, and if you haven't read any of his work yet, you really need to fix that.

Now, about those Ba'is. The creatures presented within this story take their name from various Native American legends. Although I drew on Native America folklore for this story, my depiction of the Ba'is is certainly a far cry from those of tribal legend, and no offense is intended in my portrayal of these insect-like creatures. Various tribes, including the Potawatomi, have stories about the Ba'is (sometimes called Pa'is or Paissa, depending on the tribe and dialect), and in most of their stories the Ba'is are much gentler creatures, more like fairies than the monstrous man-eaters I've depicted here. Sometimes, though... Sometimes, these little creatures can pose a threat to humans, especially if provoked...

Finally, many, many thanks to you for reading my work. I hope we meet again soon.

ABOUT THE AUTHOR

Michael Patrick Hicks is the author of a number of speculative fiction titles. His debut novel, *Convergence*, was an Amazon Breakthrough Novel Award 2013 Quarter-Finalist. His most recent works are *Mass Hysteria*, a horror novel, and *Broken Shells*, a horror novella.

He has written for the Audiobook Reviewer and Graphic Novel Reporter websites, in addition to working as a freelance journalist and news photographer.

In between compulsively buying books and adding titles that he does not have time for to his Netflix queue, he is hard at work on his next story.

Website:
http://michaelpatrickhicks.com

E-Mail: mphicks@michaelpatrickhicks.com

CHECK OUT THESE OTHER TITLES FROM

HIGH FEVER BOOKS

"Fun, horrible fun, from start to finish."
Horror Novel Reviews

It came from space...

Something virulent. Something evil. Something new. And it is infecting the town of Falls Breath.

Carried to Earth in a freak meteor shower, an alien virus has infected the animals. Pets and wildlife have turned rabid, attacking without warning. Dogs and cats terrorize their owners, while deer and wolves from the neighboring woods hunt in packs, stalking and killing their human prey without mercy.

As the town comes under siege, Lauren searches for her

boyfriend, while her policeman father fights to restore some semblance of order against a threat unlike anything he has seen before. The Natural Order has been upended completely, and nowhere is safe.

…and it is spreading.

Soon, the city will find itself in the grips of mass hysteria.

To survive, humanity will have to fight tooth and nail.

> **"*Revolver* is some of the angriest fiction I've ever read. ... An incendiary short story fueled by rage and written with style."**
> **Kyle Warner, author of *Rakasa***

Cara Stone is a broken woman: penniless, homeless, and hopeless. When given the chance to appear on television, she jumps at the opportunity to win a minimum of $5,000 for her family.

The state-run, crowdfunded series, Revolver, has been established by the nation's moneyed elite to combat the increasing plight of class warfare.

There's never been a Revolver contestant quite like Cara before. The corporate states of America are hungry for blood, and she promises to deliver.

**FOR FANS OF H.P. LOVECRAFT AND *ALIEN*
COMES
A NEW WORK OF COSMIC TERROR!**

"A sharp, crackling exploration of man's hubris and science gone wrong. This is Frankenstein for the new millennium."
Hunter Shea, author of *We Are Always Watching* and *The Jersey Devil*

Inside an abandoned mining station, in the depths of space, a team of scientists are seeking to unravel the secrets of humanity's origin. Using cutting-edge genetic cloning experiments, their discoveries take them down an unimaginable and frightening path as their latest creation proves to be far more than they had bargained for.